Triangles

by

T. E. Parker

Eloquent Books

Eloquent Books
An imprint of Strategic Book Group
P.O. Box 333
Durham CT 06422
www.StrategicBookGroup.com

ISBN: 978-1-60860-980-2

Printed in the United States of America

Book Design: SP

Acknowledgements

I would like to thank my friend and work colleague, Lee Adams, for the sound advice he has given me on a number of occasions but particularly with regard to having this novel published.

I would also like to express my gratitude to Katy Mannering-Clarke, for reading and editing the manuscript at such short notice, my son, Andrew, for his enthusiasm and support, and my long-suffering husband, David, for his love and belief in me.

Finally, I would like to express my appreciation and thanks to my Agents and Publisher for their patience and efforts on my behalf and for giving me the opportunity to realise a dream.

"By all means marry;

if you have a good wife, you'll become happy;

if you have a bad one, you'll become a philosopher."

~Socrates

Prologue

The theatre doors opened after the last performance for the evening and people spilled out onto the street, laughing and chatting. It took several minutes for the crowd to disperse, leaving a solitary couple still standing on the steps enjoying the cool night air. They appeared to be in no great hurry, even when they eventually set off arm in arm.

"You're very quiet."

"Mmm, still thinking about the play. The writer really seems to have understood the complexities of love affairs, don't you think? He must have known a woman just like that to have been able to portray her so well emotionally. Men always insist they don't understand the way women think, but I'm beginning to believe sometimes they do!"

"Actually the play is thought to be based on the author's own experience of a relationship that ended in tragedy, except his lover was a man; the playwright was homosexual. Didn't you read the program?"

"I don't think it matters all that much really. I don't believe that kind of all-consuming passion is gendered. I suppose it must matter to some people, though, or he wouldn't have written the character as a woman."

"Well, don't forget he was writing at a time when homosexuality was illegal! But I agree with you entirely: love is indiscriminate and nobody can really help who they fall for."

He paused in the middle of the deserted street. "You being here now means the world to me; you know that, don't you?"

"Okay. So prove it," the woman replied playfully, turning away from him. "I think it's time."

"One day you'll regret teasing me..."

"I don't think so. As you said, you can't help who you fall in love with, so you may as well just give in."

"That wasn't quite what I meant, and you know it, you little minx..."

"No, please don't tickle me; I haven't the energy to run." She quickly kissed his cheek. "When we get back I want to read some more of your work. It's so different from anything I've ever seen before."

The man smiled to himself. They walked on companionably into the night.

Chapter One

I opened my eyes and she was there – Kelly! Not the Kelly I last remembered seeing some five years previous, a dull and listless shade of her former vibrant self, but the original sparkling girl she had been when we first met. She stood now, by the bedroom window, hand resting lightly on the blue marbled curtain, pulled to one side, allowing the first grey streak of dawn to slither through the cold glass. The shaft of pale light brushed past her, to rest on the duvet in a long triangular shape. There was no warmth and yet I had woken, or thought I had, disturbed by the slight change in the darkness. Now, looking into Kelly's questioning eyes, I decided that I must be dreaming. I couldn't move, didn't want to disturb or destroy what I felt certain to be the fragile remnant of a wistful dream. She smiled, and my eyes caught the soft falling of the curtain fabric, and then she was gone. I struggled upright, my tired eyes stinging, fully awake now and terribly aware of the continued gentle sway of the heavy curtain, disturbed by no breeze from outside; the window had been shut tight against the sharp night air before I'd retired for the night. I scrambled out of bed and across the room, pulling both curtains open to peer down at the silent road below.

Street lamps still burned yellow, the sickly light providing little illumination. However, the early morning sun, as yet hidden by the houses across the street, brightened the sky enough to reveal a man standing quite still on the pavement adjacent to the house. He reminded me of a matchstick person from one of Lowry's paintings for he seemed, even from my elevated position, to be incredibly tall and thin. Instinctively I drew back, for although his raised face was not distinguishable in the weak light as anybody I recognised, he appeared to be watching my window. It was mere seconds before I peered back out again but in common with Kelly, the man had now vanished.

I opened the window and leaned out to search up and down the deserted street. A cat padded out into the road from beneath a parked car, and the downstairs window in the house opposite mine lit up as the occupants prepared for another day. I drew back inside, firmly shutting out the sound of the dawn chorus, and slouched back across the room to sit heavily on the bed, rubbing my face, thinking. I reached over to switch on my bedside lamp, found my glasses, together with the notebook and biro kept on the cabinet, and glanced at my watch. It was 6:18 a.m. and I noted down the date and time in the book, adding: *Waking dream – Kelly in bedroom – Stranger on street.* Then I went to get ready for work, considering all the while whether I'd dreamt up some sort of private detective to watch the house because I still couldn't accept that my wife had left without warning or explanation. Perhaps the man was a metaphor for my desire to solve the mystery and make everything right.

As usual my breakfast was a nondescript affair involving a cereal bar and two digestive biscuits, dunked in coffee, whilst standing in the draughty kitchen. (My mother would disapprove both the 'meal' and the kitchen, but I told myself I didn't care.) I hurried from the house, stuffing papers into my briefcase as I went and firmly pulling the front door shut behind me. I always turned the key twice to ensure it had not only latched but was doubly locked; I had always been security conscious – paranoid Kelly used to tease. *Kelly again – haunting me as usual.* I slung my case onto the back seat of my mini then discovered with dismay that I had a puncture. The school where I taught was a reasonably short distance away, so I decided there was nothing for it but to walk. Perhaps it would clear my head a little and calm the inevitable concerns about the day ahead. I was grateful that I hadn't brought work home and had no books to carry.

The caretaker, Kenny, peered out from the confined space, next to the drama cupboard, which he claimed as his own and called his "Good morning" as I strode purposefully down the corridor from the main entrance. I lifted an arm in acknowledgment and congratulated myself for arriving early, while most of the building was still quiet and deserted. Kenny wouldn't disturb my work as he was enjoying his early morning tea break, reading his newspaper, having already made his first rounds of the school grounds.

It was going to be a busy week, I mused; there was the annual school performance looming next month and I needed some time to organise rehearsals. I intended recruiting my cast from members of the enthusiastic little drama club, I had established last year, rather than selecting my actors from the ranks of year 6 as had been the tradition in the past. I also wanted to set up the equipment for a science lesson that morning so that I'd be ready to begin the children on a series of experiments with regard to changing materials, straight after registration. However, as I reached my classroom I found the Head, Brian Cooke, waiting for me. He was perched easily on the edge of my desk, casually flicking through the stack of unmarked exercise books I'd left there.

"Peter!" He greeted me pleasantly, as if surprised and glad to see me. My heart sank. "I've just had Mr. and Mrs. Jenkins on the telephone, wanting to see me about Thomas; how's he been behaving? They've been having problems with him at home and wondered if it was in any way related to anything going on here."

He waited patiently as I placed my briefcase on the floor of the resources cupboard and hung my jacket on the inside of the door.

"Actually I was coming to see you first thing…"

The conversation really only took twenty minutes or so as we discussed the behavioural problems of the ten year old boy in question. Thomas Jenkins had only been in my class for three months, having been transferred from another primary school which had excluded him for bullying. He was a challenging child, rarely prepared to stay on task during lessons and often distracting and picking arguments with other pupils. It was obvious he had some kind of learning difficulties, and these in turn affected his self-esteem, so I had tried very hard to be patient. However, he had been particularly trying the previous day and I had eventually warned him that I'd be speaking to his parents. He swore defiantly and marched from the classroom just as the last bell of the day sounded and his classmates, shocked into silence by the sudden outburst, left school somewhat subdued. I had surreptitiously followed Thomas to the gate and observed him as he met his mother. He had, by that time, appeared completely unperturbed, taking the bag of crisps she offered him and calling to another pupil as they left the school. I watched as the boys departed, chatting and jostling one another, followed by the weary Mrs. Jenkins. I had then retreated unseen back to the classroom. I wasn't about to give up on the boy yet, and although the warning about contacting his parents hadn't been an idle threat, I wanted to think about how to best manage the situation to move forward before doing so.

I explained all this to the Head now and I was relieved to find, when I had explained the circumstances leading up to the incident, Brian was sympathetic and supportive. He agreed with my conclusion and suggested it might be in order to arrange a joint meeting with both parents and the school psychologist as soon as possible. He left to ring Mr. and Mrs. Jenkins and I began to set up the classroom for Science. There was no time for considering arrangements for the school play now – that would have to wait until lunchtime. As it was I would have to spend the morning thinking on my feet. I felt tired and depressed.

**

"Not really ready for the auditions Wednesday, are you?" Caroline Lyman sidled up to me as I made a mug of tea in the little staffroom kitchenette at break-time.

"Oh, I'll be ready. I just need to get a bit more organised, as usual," I muttered irritably.

"I thought I'd help out. I had Year 4 design and paint posters during Art this morning – to inform the kids how they can audition."

"Posters? Great idea. Thanks."

"You can choose which two you prefer, and I could stick them up for you at lunchtime."

"Why don't you choose for me? I trust your judgment and it would help me out – I've a stack of marking to do."

"Okay." I could tell she was pleased. "I promised prizes for one boy and one girl to make it fair – well, it's best to be politically correct, isn't it? I thought we could display one poster at the entrance to the hall and the other near the library. I think you'll be pleasantly surprised at some of the art work – it's really quite good. That should leave you time for a quick drink with me at the Knight's Arms after school."

For some as yet unfathomable reason, Caroline reminded me of my mother; both women would be considered smart, ambitious and handsome, rather than beautiful, but there the likeness ended. Caroline came from a family of teachers and had married one of the lecturers from the university she'd attended. As I understood it, the marriage wasn't working out and the couple had separated because her husband was so absorbed in his own career that he had little time for, or indeed interest in, anything else. My mother, on the other hand, had come from money. By her mid-twenties she had been a success in her own right, a much sought after artistic designer working freelance in the textile industry. She married my father, a young, charismatic Anglican vicar, after meeting at a family party and, to everyone's amazement, abandoned her career in favour of a much more genteel existence in an affluent, leafy, rural parish.

My father was well-liked but not ambitious and declined several promotions offered by the Church over the years, claiming it would interfere with his family life and all that he really enjoyed about his work; he liked people, was comfortable socialising and mixing with those from all walks of life but appeared to have little interest in the institution, hierarchy, or material fabric of the Church. My mother accepted this while my sister and I were children, playing the part of a country vicar's wife with aplomb, using her artistic talents for the humble pursuits of flower arranging and leading embroidery groups or catering for garden parties. This afforded my sister and me a fairly carefree and happy childhood.

11

However, when I left home to study, that all changed. My sister met and fell in love with a salesman, shortly after I left, and moved north to be with him, and suddenly my father's career and social status became much more important to my mother. Perhaps she'd been playing the martyr for all the preceding years, I don't know, but she began to nag and push for my father to 'improve' himself, her demands becoming more insistent until her arguments eventually culminated in threats of divorce. I'm pretty sure she wasn't in the least concerned about money, and she showed no inclination to re-commence her own career. I just think she rather fancied herself married to a bishop or at least a dean but she didn't get her own way.

My father was a mild-mannered man, and though he must have loved my mother dearly, he disliked pressure so eventually he abandoned her, left the church and took up landscape gardening. I still can't work out whether I feel respect or contempt for his solution to the problem.

Oddly enough, despite my enviable upbringing, I have never been particularly close to either of my parents; we were never a demonstrative family. One of the things I had always admired about my wife, Kelly, was the way she expressed all feelings with complete honesty and a total lack of restraint.

As for my colleague's similarity to my mother, well I couldn't see Caroline either giving up her own career for spouse and family, or attempting to enjoy success vicariously through her partner. All the same, I was aware that her interest in me was something more than that of a colleague, and the feeling wasn't mutual, so I didn't want to encourage her. I was therefore searching frantically for an excuse that wouldn't offend, when Brian stuck his head round the door.

"Sorry to interrupt, Peter. Can I have a quick word in my office?"

I nodded then smiled wanly at Caroline and tried to achieve a balance of appearing disappointed but not too much so.

"I'm a bit tied up tonight, analysing the rest of the English test results, sorry." I shrugged and beat a hasty retreat in the Head teacher's wake, without waiting for her to suggest a rain-check.

"Shut the door, Peter; I'm afraid I've some bad news." Brian removed his glasses and began to wipe them – never a good sign.

"Is it about Jenkins?" I could barely keep the apprehension from my voice; I'd been pretty strict with the boy recently but didn't believe I'd overdone it.

"No, that's fine. I'll let you know the date of the meeting when it's been finalised. I've just had the police on the telephone. I'm afraid you've been burgled."

I stared at him in silent astonishment: security conscious I might be, but the news was a complete shock. Unbidden, an image of the stranger in the street flashed into my mind, but I dismissed it as no more than a fragment of a dream.

"Why would anyone want to break into *my* house? I haven't exactly got much worth stealing!"

"You'd better take the rest of the day off and sort things out; Jane is already organising supply cover," he looked towards the school's reception office. "I understand the police have secured the house, but you need to call in at the station. Apparently there's been some sort of accident…"

Two hours later I stood, arms folded, watching the mechanics supervising the hoisting of my mini onto the back of a breakdown truck. The accident, I had discovered on reaching the police station, had been the obliteration of the passenger side of my car; somebody had ploughed into it and continued on driving without stopping. The mini would be a write-off, as far as the insurers were concerned; the bodywork looked beyond repair and there had, as far as I knew, been no witnesses to the accident.

The damage had been discovered by my neighbour, Jeremy Scott (affectionately known in the neighbourhood as Jem), when he'd returned home from his night shift at the paper mill on the other side of town. He had picked up the wing mirror and various other bits of wreckage from the middle of the road and had taken them to place near my doorstep, intending to push a note through the letterbox, when he discovered my front door ajar. He pushed it open, calling out, thinking perhaps I was inside instead of at work. It was then he found furniture turned upside down, some smashed and with torn upholstery; there was graffiti scrawled across the lounge walls in green paint, which had dripped and splattered onto the carpet, and books, papers and other possessions were strewn all over the place. If it hadn't been for the car, the state of the house might have gone undiscovered until my return from school that evening, although the police felt the accident with the car and the house break-in were possibly two unconnected incidents. They said that I was probably just unlucky.

Unlucky – that was an understatement! At least the second floor of my home seemed undisturbed, although I reasoned it might have been difficult for the police to tell if the burglar had been upstairs: the bedroom was as I'd left it that morning, bed still unmade and clothes scattered on the floor. I never had been particularly tidy. However, I decided I couldn't face clearing up that night and I accepted the offer of supper and a bed in the spare room at Jem's house. I'd hesitated at first, thinking of Kelly. Supposing she came and I wasn't there? Then I realised how ridiculous I was being. Dreams, if persistent, would haunt the creator wherever he went, or if he was sufficiently distracted, leave him alone for the night. *She could be a ghost...* the thought slithered unwelcome into my mind and with cold deliberation I crushed the notion. For Kelly to be a spirit, if indeed such things existed, she would have to be dead and I was a long way from accepting that. No, I didn't believe in spectres – well not in Kelly's ghost anyway.

Jem and his wife, Eva, joined me in the street as the garage truck pulled away, my car secured on the back. We watched together as the vehicle turned the corner of the street then Jem handed me a bundle of correspondence.

"I picked up the post from your hall. There are a few spots of paint on one or two of the envelopes and a boot-mark, but apart from that I saw no reason to give them to the police."

"Thanks."

I shuffled through the various letters – junk mail mostly, a gas bill and one pale blue envelope, handwritten in black ink. I felt the blood sing in my ears as I recognised the handwriting. I tore at the envelope to open it, oblivious of my neighbours' curious glances. A single sheet of matching pale blue paper, unfolded impatiently, revealed the opening words:

'*My dearest Peter,*

I am writing in the hope that you will help me, as I have nobody else to whom I can turn. Please forgive me; I have no choice but to write…'

Jem placed a firm hand on my shoulder, nodding his head towards his house as, still in shock, I looked up from Kelly's neat hand.

"Come on lad, Eva's brewed a nice pot of tea. You need to get off your feet by the looks of things."

I nodded in agreement, stuffing paper and envelope deep into my trouser pocket, where they seemed to press warmly against my thigh. I binned the rest of the mail on the way through my neighbours' gate. Jem grinned.

"Wish I had the balls to do that with my bills!"

I just grunted an acknowledgment, following him over the front doorstep and into his hall, my mind still dazed by the fact that Kelly had written to me. In the five years she had been missing I had never given her up as lost forever. Now she appeared to need my help! Every nerve in my body seemed to be urging me to read the rest of her writing immediately, yet something else held me back and I told myself it was common sense. If it had been a real emergency she would have telephoned or visited. A spitefully insidious voice whispered, somewhere in the back of my mind, '*She wants a divorce at last, to make this separation legally binding,'* but I ignored it. No, I decided, the letter could wait until I had some privacy when I went to bed. I'd had enough drama for one day and I badly needed that cup of tea. I gratefully accepted the proffered mug from Eva's hand and took a chair at the kitchen table.

In retrospect, I sometimes wonder how I managed to get through the evening without excusing myself and going to the bathroom or somewhere, just to discover what Kelly had to say. What could be important enough to necessitate corresponding, yet in so few words that one small sheet of notepaper would suffice? Even more astonishing is the fact that, after participating in small talk and gossip, while eating a hearty meal of steak and kidney pie and vegetables, followed by treacle tart and ice cream, washed down by several cans of larger, I finally left the Scotts in front of their television set watching some police drama, brushed my teeth and tumbled into bed in their spare room without even thinking anymore about the letter. I had fallen at once into a deep sleep and woke the next morning to find the fresh set of clothes, I'd pulled untidily from my overnight bag the previous evening whilst retrieving my pyjamas, neatly pressed and draped carefully over the chair. A mug of tea was set on the bedside table. I had heard nobody enter the room, and looking at my watch, I saw that it was already 7:45 a.m. I groaned aloud, aware that I was probably going to be late for work. Jem rapped on my door at that moment then opened it, peering at my disgruntled face.

"We didn't wake you, Son, it being Saturday. Eva said that you looked all in. We'll be off to the supermarket in a little while. Your breakfast is keeping warm under a plate on the hob. We shouldn't be too long but if you want to get on at your place, take the backdoor key. That way you'll be able to get back in here, if you need to."

I lay back against the pillows with a sigh of gratitude; I'd forgotten it was the weekend. I thanked Jem and promised I'd be up shortly. He assured me there was no hurry then closed the door behind him and I listened to his slippered feet descending the stairs. I couldn't believe I'd slept such a heavy and dreamless sleep in a bed that was not my own. It was then that I remembered Kelly's letter and leaned over the side of the bed, groping around the floor for the slacks I'd worn the previous day. Puzzled, I found nothing but empty carpet and then a thought began to take form, gradually filling me with unease. Eva, so tidy and maternal, was probably even now loading the washing machine. I threw the bedclothes aside, hastily pulled on the fresh clothes and was still fumbling with buttons as I hurried to the top of the stairs.

"Eva, my trousers! Where are my trousers from yesterday?"

Chapter Two

Eva and Jem had, of course, already left for the shops and my worst fears were realised as I recognised my clothes tumbling around this way and that as the washing machine obeyed its programmed cycle. I looked at the electronic display and realised with despair that I would be unable to unlock the door for at least 45 minutes and even if I managed it, flooding the kitchen in the process, the letter would already be ruined by now. There was little I could do, so I sat down to the eggs, bacon and toast that had been left for me.

Twenty minutes later I was standing in my own ruined front room with a black plastic sack, surveying the mess. I had confirmed that there was nothing of any value missing when the police had asked me to check the house contents the previous day, and as I crouched down to gather up the pieces of a broken clock, I wondered what drove people to such mindless destruction. I glanced up at the wall daubed with paint, trying once again to make sense of the graffiti. It was neither letters nor numbers; it was not even a picture, but looked to be a kind of horizontal line with several wavy lines protruding from it. I shrugged and continued rummaging through the chaos strewn across the floor, thinking that the odd design must be some sort of 'tag'.

I picked up my well thumbed, dog-eared but long neglected copy of Shakespeare's plays and opened it sadly. A soft, yellowing piece of paper slid from between the pages and once again I recognised Kelly's handwriting. I caught the paper as it fell; I'd forgotten this:

Dear Peter,

I have tried very hard to make things right between us because I have always valued your friendship, but to be honest I'm beginning to be tired of your cold indifference. Surely I am entitled to express my opinion without worrying about you taking offence indefinitely! I have shown you that I am willing to accept your assessment of my acting abilities, yet you have ignored all of my attempts to re-establish the comfortable, easygoing relationship we had before.

I keep praying – it's all I seem to have left to do that might help. Please speak to me soon.

Kelly

My mind flew back over the years to the time before we were married, before we were even romantically involved.

Kelly had been a student at the local grammar school and I had been asked to help my friend, April Harper, head of the drama department there, to stage a production of *A Midsummer Night's Dream*. I was in my early twenties, still wet behind the ears from teacher training college, and Kelly at eighteen, preparing for her A' levels had caught my attention during rehearsals. She was my vision of Hermia, slight and dark with rich, brown curls that she often wore piled on the top of her head. She had a small, heart-shaped face yet her chin was firm and stubborn and her dark eyes glittered with quick intelligence. She hadn't put herself forward for a part in the play but had signed up to help with painting the scenery while her boyfriend auditioned for Demetrius. To be fair, she had an invaluable artistic flair, which was more than welcome during the preparations for the drama, and it had taken some effort to persuade her that she could and indeed should act.

To this day, I could swear, hand on heart, that I had no amorous inclinations towards Kelly at the time whatsoever; my interest had been purely professional. This is not simply a love story but something far more intriguing. One might even describe the events I intend to relate as both mysterious and mystical but I digress.

Once she overcame the initial 'stage fright' it was obvious Kelly was a natural actor. She progressed quickly and often helped the other students grow into their characters. At first we got on really well, seeming to share the same dry sense of humour, and she became increasingly confident to the point where she was putting forward suggestions about delivery of speeches and stage management.

Sometimes she couldn't make rehearsals – I never really found out why – and the girl previously cast as Hermia, who'd been demoted to understudy in favour of Kelly, filled in. The understudy, Marcia, hadn't really minded at all that Kelly had eclipsed her on stage, since she'd found learning the script a great deal harder than she had anticipated. On such occasions Kelly would arrive ten minutes or so towards the end of a rehearsal and indulge in constructive criticism. Sometimes I would find little notes from her clipped to my copy of the play, particularly with regard to her own reading of Hermia's portrayal. My colleague, April, thought it amusing at first, but she gradually became irritated and began to make the odd sarcastic remark about who was really directing. I was beginning to feel a little put out myself, particularly when Kelly's boyfriend, Tony, alias Demetrius, began to exhibit signs of jealousy towards me and became sullen and un-cooperative.

One day things came to a head when Kelly interrupted Hypolyta's reply to Theseus concerning his eagerness for their wedding, jumping up on the stage to make her point more forcibly.

"For Heaven's sake, Gina, the woman would be subdued and miserable – she's being forced into a marriage by the defeat of her people during battle!"

"Actually, I disagree," I interrupted firmly, approaching the stage. "Hypolyta would be haughty and proud as befits a warrior queen, despite her situation. Later, her posture and facial expressions, behind the Duke's back, can reveal her contempt at his appraisal of Hermia's situation, making the audience laugh; this *is* a comedy after all." I deliberately addressed Gina with a nod, completely avoiding all eye contact with Kelly. Kelly left the theatre without a word. April joined me as the students dispersed.

"It's about time you put her in her place," she congratulated me, smiling her approval.

"Ahh, she means well, but I think she was getting a little too bossy."

To my surprise, the following morning the school secretary came to my classroom with a note. Kelly apologised profusely for interfering with my work. She hoped that I would join her for coffee at Joe's, the little cafe across the road from the grammar school, at half past four that afternoon to show there were no hard feelings and that we could still be friends. Jane Curtis eyed me severely, as I frowned at the message, and told me that a youth was waiting in reception for a reply. I scribbled on a bright yellow jotter:

Hi Kelly,

No problem – I know you were only trying to help. Hermia is coming along fine. I'm busy this afternoon – staff meeting. Then I have to pick up some groceries. See you next week at rehearsal, as usual.

I added my initials, tore off the small page and folded it, before passing it to the secretary. I knew she wouldn't be able to resist taking a peek, but there was nothing private in the note. I had been faintly amused at the idea of Kelly thinking us friends, yet didn't want to offend her by treating her as a child and risk losing one of the lead players with only 3 weeks left before the first night of the play.

The following week Kelly didn't show up for rehearsal. Tony gruffly handed me another message, which April read over my shoulder.

Hi Peter,

So sorry I can't make tonight. I really would be there if I could because I'm a bit concerned about the scene where Helena and Hermia argue in the woods – it still doesn't feel right somehow. Would you have time to meet up and talk about it Saturday morning?

I'd be free between 10 and 11, and I know school's open because I've agreed to help with moving some of the props. Anyway, let me know.

Kelly

"I think someone has a crush, don't you?" April murmured, reading over my shoulder. "Careful, Peter, these things can get out of hand…"

"Don't fuss, April. I can look out for myself." I dashed off a reply on the blank bottom half of a page of my script.

Kelly,

Don't worry; I'm sure it will all come right before the big night. Family christening Saturday: I will be out of town all weekend. I'm not really looking forward to the drive – I've been so busy at school and writing reports that I'm quite tired. Keep practising. I know you will not let us down.

PK

I was quite relieved to see Kelly at the next rehearsal, although her heart didn't appear to be in the acting. She intoned her words clearly but Hermia's exasperation was more like resignation, and the spirited words assigned to her during her spat with Helena lacked conviction. I asked to see Kelly at the end of the session and enquired whether all was well. To my horror she started to cry. I hurried her into the school kitchen at the back of the hall, aware of the inquisitive glances from departing pupils. It *would* have to be the one day April couldn't stay behind. I offered the weeping girl my handkerchief and leaned back on the stainless steel work surface, several feet away from her, feeling awkward and uncomfortably out of my depth but determined not to show it. I listened silently as she blurted out her troubles.

Her father was being transferred to the Manchester branch of his company, and her parents had put their home on the market and were making preparations to move. They had arranged for Kelly's aunt to take her in, if necessary, so that she could complete her examinations, then they expected her to apply to the university in Manchester. They weren't really too concerned about her choice of academic study, although they assumed she would have an interest in a career in journalism: Kelly had been a keen contributor to the school newspaper for several years, even taking a turn at editorship. It didn't surprise me, somehow. Kelly was a girl of many talents and seemed to throw herself wholeheartedly into whatever she became involved with. However, journalism apparently wasn't her ambition. Kelly didn't want to go to university; she had her heart set on the art college at Canterbury, an aspiration her affluent middle-class parents couldn't understand. They blamed it on the friends she'd recently become involved with. I presumed this included Tony, but as if she read my mind, she blew her nose noisily and said, "They approve of Tony, you know. He's going into banking. They don't even seem to mind that he's started hinting about getting engaged!"

"Oh, congratulations…"

"Don't be ridiculous. I'm only eighteen. Why on earth should I be thinking about tying myself down before I've had a chance to taste all the things life has to offer?"

I bit my lip in an effort not to grin. The sentiments were certainly adult, but she sounded like a petulant child. I cleared my throat.

"Very wise. I expect you hope to travel – see the world and have a career before you settle down."

She looked up at me scornfully and sniffed. "I've been abroad as much as I want to for the time being, thank you very much. My parents have taken me all over the world on holiday, and they aren't the type to settle for lying on a beach. They love to explore and 'enjoy the culture'." She raised her fore-fingers, bending them quickly a couple of times to indicate quotation marks, my balled hanky secured behind one thumb. "Italy has been a favourite for the last couple of years. Then they wonder why I'm passionate about art! And don't look at me like that!" She glared accusingly, eyes flashing with passion, "I know what you're thinking – four star hotels and package holidays aren't the same as travelling with

24

a rucksack and staying at youth hostels. Well, that's not my idea of fun. Why refuse yourself home comforts if you don't have to? You just deny people jobs in the service industries."

She sniffed again and I was relieved to see the tears gone as she stuffed my now quite soggy handkerchief into her raincoat pocket.

"I've been learning how other people live all over this planet for years. They even take you on little tours to show you inside one of the native's homes in the Dominican Republic, you know – let you get an idea of the poverty and simplicity of life there. No, what I want to do is discover more about myself and who I am, before I give up my identity to become somebody's spouse and mother. Is that so selfish?"

"Kelly, why don't you talk to Miss Harper tomorrow? Maybe she could make an appointment with your parents and you could all sit down and discuss things."

"Your friend, April Harper, isn't interested. All she cares about at the moment is this stupid play. She just told me to go see the school counsellor."

"Well that *is* the school counsellor's job…"

"Yeah, but *she's* having a difficult pregnancy and is on indefinite sick leave. It could be months before I get to talk to anybody. Don't worry. I don't expect you to do anything. I'll sort something out."

She picked up her school bag, which she'd let fall to the floor during her bout of weeping. "Thanks for listening." She turned to go but then hesitated, turning back to look me straight in the eye. "I like you Peter – I think you know that. I know there can't be anything serious between us because you're a teacher and I'm a student but I would appreciate your friendship, you know?"

I stared at the ground with a wry smile, feeling the colour flame in my face. I was flattered, of course, but I had to nip this in the bud. I fumbled for an appropriate reply such as "Don't call me Peter" or "I don't think that's a good idea" but was unsure how to take the sting out of the rejection and let her down gently.

"That's very mature of you to realise…" I began but she was already gone.

You might think my relationship with Kelly developed from then but you'd be wrong. In an old black and white movie I would probably try hard to control my passion for the beautiful starlet, who later goes on to become a legendary actress. She would, of course, be discovered by a famous film producer, who just happened to be at the school production. I would suffer for years, a broken man taken to abusing alcohol. I would lose my job and mope in a shabby apartment, until a friend persuaded me to help with a play at the same school, the reason being that the proceeds were going to the local children's hospice where his child lay dying. The child would suddenly find the will to fight for his life because he wanted to see the performance. The heroine would somehow hear of my generosity and courage and on the first night would return, at last, for me to take her into my arms and declare my undying love.

In a modern teen flick or musical perhaps the school production itself would be the motivating force behind our attraction for one another, and after overcoming various obstacles designed to impede rather than prevent our relationship, I would be poised in the wings, on the first night, waiting to announce my feelings to her as she left the stage, flushed with the success of a glittering performance. We wouldn't realise somebody had raised the curtains, as I knelt to propose on stage and we'd be applauded and approved by audience and actors alike, and the after-performance party would become an engagement celebration.

I muse on these possibilities of a storyline purely because I had written a few short plays by that time and was forever searching for the original slant on a story. However, I should explain that this story is no romantic comedy composed for entertainment.

I sighed as I now reconsidered the events that followed the spring term of that year, while I pressed the faded yellow note from Kelly back between the pages of the book. I replaced the heavy tome with several others on a shelf, stuffing those books too damaged to repair into the black sack. Remembering helped pass the time and take my mind off the chore as I patiently and methodically waded through my jumbled possessions.

Even as a young man I was cautious and sometimes anxious, despite the confidence I then had in my aptitude for teaching. Early in the evening, on the day of Kelly's conversation with me in the school kitchen, I rang April Harper and gave her a rough outline of what had happened and all that Kelly had told me about her problems and hope for our friendship. I told April I would not be spending much more time at the grammar school, my job being all but done anyway, and she agreed that it was probably for the best.

As it happened, I didn't even get to attend that performance of *A Midsummer Night's Dream*, although I was later told that everything went without a hitch for the full week of its staging and that it had been reasonably well received. Directly I put the receiver down, after talking to April, the telephone rang and I found myself listening to the cracked and hopeless voice of my brother-in-law. He was calling, he told me, because my sister wasn't in a fit state to do so herself. My new baby nephew, whose baptism I had recently attended, had just become a victim of 'cot-death syndrome'. I agreed to drive to Birmingham to be with the bereaved parents just as soon as I could arrange leave from work.

I rang Brian Cook immediately after my brother-in-law severed the connection. I was touched by Brian's sympathetic response and I made a point of popping into school next morning in order to thank him, before I left on my four hour drive. I tapped his office door and entered without waiting to be summonsed, expecting to find him still sorting through the morning mail, and was a little disconcerted to be confronted by two men in dark suits, one seated across from Brian on the other side of his desk, the other standing legs astride, hands behind his back looking for all the world like an undertaker. Their eyes seemed to bore into me as Brian welcomed me, introducing the two men as police officers.

"Peter is the teacher you were asking about," Brian told the seated policeman, before turning back to me.

"Apparently one of the pupils from Greenacres didn't go home last night after the play rehearsal, Peter, a young woman we've been led to believe you've worked with and know quite well – Kelly Butler."

Chapter Three

I looked from Brian to the seated policeman, then to the other before returning my gaze to Brian who cleared his throat and continued his explanation to me.

"We're all particularly concerned, Peter, because two other young women have been reported missing in the vicinity of the school over the past couple of weeks. The police have spoken briefly to the Head at Greenacres this morning and have already interviewed your friend, Miss Harper. It seems you were probably the last person to speak to the girl before she left the grammar school." Brian took off his glasses and began to polish the lenses with his handkerchief meticulously.

"I'm sure you'll understand we have to take this matter seriously-time may be of the essence. We'll be talking to pupils, particularly Miss Butler's friends in the drama group, later on this morning, but we just have a few questions for you first, if you wouldn't mind helping us with our enquiries. Do sit down Mr. Kendall." The officer relinquished his chair, offering it to me. "Of course, it's quite feasible that the girl will turn up at any moment, but since there appears to be no reason for her to leave home, no argument with her parents, and she left no note and hasn't telephoned, the circumstances surrounding her disappearance seem a little suspicious."

In consternation, I slumped down in the now empty seat almost without thinking. I then, of course, felt myself to be at a distinct psychological disadvantage, as the officer towered over me and was even more intimidating than ever, but I took a deep breath, stared at the floor and spoke resolutely.

"That's not entirely true – about the lack of problems at home," I assured him. "Kelly was quite upset during rehearsals and spoke to me afterwards about her parents moving to Manchester. I believe there was some disagreement about her choice of future study?"

I looked up in time to intercept the glance between the two policemen.

"Mr. Kendall, is it true that Miss Butler is infatuated with you?"

It was the first time I'd heard the 'undertaker' talk, and the question seemed a little like an accusation. I answered warily, explaining everything that had occurred at the play rehearsals, about the notes which had passed between Kelly and me, and finally about the telephone conversation with April, concerning my decision to spend less time at Greenacres henceforth.

To my relief the policemen appeared satisfied. They thanked me for my assistance, apologised to Brian for any inconvenience their visit might have caused then, shaking our hands politely, they left.

I don't remember much about the drive to Birmingham or the days that followed spent with my family. Baby Charlie's funeral and the aftermath now seem to merge into a dreary, dark memory of aching sadness. I had been granted extended leave of a little over three weeks, with Brian's blessing, since my sister suffered a complete nervous breakdown.

During this time Kelly was missing for six days. I'd all but forgotten her disappearance and my meeting with the police by the time I returned to school. Apparently, April told me later, Kelly had turned up on the evening of the first performance and had insisted on taking part. Her parents had reluctantly agreed but were frustrated and upset because she had refused to say where she had been, who she had been with and why she'd stayed away from home. I was intrigued, of course, but puzzled over the matter for little more than a few minutes as I listened to April. We then moved onto a discussion about the local amateur dramatics society, and I dismissed Kelly from my mind without a second thought.

I soon slotted back into school routine and Brian seemed pleased to see me back, although that probably had more to do with not having to organise or pay for any further supply teachers for my class than anything else. Life went on much the same as it always had. I met an attractive brunette, Grace Johnson, at a friend's party and began dating her. She was a professional musician, a violinist, five years older than me but excellent company. I attended concerts with her and she joined me on theatre trips in London, and the friendship quickly evolved into a sexual relationship as it became a habit for me to stay over at her apartment.

I fancied myself falling in love and began looking in estate agents' windows back home whenever I went into the local town centre. The property market was almost as inaccessible to fairly new teachers in those days as it is today, but I had been left some money by a great uncle, on my mother's side of the family, and I intended to put it to good use.

Somerbourne, the town I'd come to think of as home, might almost be considered part of the Swale district, being situated approximately four miles from the Medway towns. Most of the original residents had been connected to, or worked in, the paper mill, which had been built in the nineteenth century near to the creek. One of my elderly neighbours once described Somerbourne as having been little more than a 'one horse town' in the days of his childhood, but it had expanded over the decades to accommodate the growing population, although the mill had ceased to be the principle employer, the service industry having taken its place in this respect. The paper mill, famous in its prime, was now behind the times, its technology outmoded. Consequently, it was struggling to compete with more modern and efficient European companies capable of producing and importing vast quantities of high quality paper, and there were often threats of the mill's closure. Every year further redundancies were announced and the number of people living on government benefits increased. However, the town continued to thrive after a fashion as more and more people found new employment, commuting by train early each morning to the Medway towns or cities of Canterbury, Rochester and even London to work during the week, but returning to spend their leisure time with their families in the comparative peace and quiet of countrified Somerbourne.

I had moved to the outskirts of Somerbourne, finding rooms in a little boarding house near to the cricket grounds, after I had been offered a job at my final teaching placement. Friends from teacher training college asked what I saw in the place since it had few of the trendy night life attractions of the larger towns and cities, yet I was quite content to live there. There were shops, a couple of large supermarkets on the edge of the town, a reasonable leisure centre and library and fairly regular public transport, should I wish to go out of town without driving. The local people have on the whole always been decent and friendly too.

The estate agents gave me plenty of ideas. The first couple of properties I looked at with a view to buying had originally been built to house employees from the mill: little terraced cottages, with tiny back yards and front doors opening directly onto the street. Then I looked at a couple of places in Parkway Road; this had been fondly referred to as 'Piano and Poverty Street' in times gone by because the people living there had more often been concerned with keeping up appearances and social status than family welfare. Residents might quietly go hungry on a regular basis, living cramped together in the backs of houses, but their front rooms were immaculate and generally boasted a highly polished piano to impress potential visitors of the affluence and respectability of the family.

Next, I looked a little further from the town centre to where the surrounding countryside had been developed over the years. I soon found a nice little semi-detached property built in the 1960s, with a small garden on a quiet street. I put a deposit down with vague notions of proposing to Grace on the anniversary of our first date for, I surmised, it would take a while and a generous portion of my modest earnings to fix the place up the way I wanted it.

I was a little naïve in those days; I'd only been seeing Grace for a little over three months but it had felt like I'd known her forever. I therefore had the shock of my life the day I exchanged contracts on my new home and travelled up to London on the evening train to tell her my news in person. I hadn't even mentioned that I was thinking of moving, up until then, or that I was considering our future together, so I really only had myself to blame.

I retrieved the spare key from its hiding place beneath the rubber plant on the third-storey landing of her apartment block and let myself into her flat. Her living room was deserted but the television set was on, the volume turned down low. I was about to call out when I heard laughter coming from the bedroom. I walked slowly to the door and placed my ear against the wood. Judging from the sounds emanating from within, I was not the only man who enjoyed Grace's company. I left quietly, replacing the key beneath the plant and retracing my steps back to the station.

I arrived at my boarding house very late and decided not to go inside and risk waking my landlady. She was a kind, motherly woman, if a little nosy, and I really didn't want to have to fend off her well-meant questions just then, so I paced the streets until I found an all-night burger bar and bought myself a cup of coffee and a cheese burger. I remember being surprised to discover that I was neither angry nor particularly heartbroken and that my appetite was as healthy as ever. I congratulated myself at how philosophical and worldly-wise I felt about the matter. In just a few short hours the whole romance with Grace seemed to have reduced itself in significance to little more than a cliché, but it had supplied the impetus for me to buy my own home and I was now looking forward to moving into the house and becoming truly independent.

I was swallowing the last few mouthfuls of coffee and contemplating buying another burger when a woman came in off the street. I glanced at her as the heavy glass plate door swung to behind her and frowned, thinking that she looked somehow familiar, yet I couldn't place where I'd seen her before. To my chagrin she approached my table instead of going to the counter as I'd expected.

"Mr. Kendall? My daughter pointed you out to me the other day as we were driving past Churchill Primary School."

I looked at her blankly.

"My daughter is Kelly Butler. I'm Maureen Butler." She offered her hand and I briefly took it in mine.

"I wonder, would it be possible for me to have a quick word?"

She sat down on the plastic chair opposite without waiting to be invited. She looked to be in her early forties, well groomed, stylish hairdo, expensive, designer clothing. I tried to smile but my face felt stiff, as if suddenly made of wood.

"First, let me tell you that I know how stubborn my daughter can be when she wants something and that I really appreciate the professional way you handled things when she became interested in you."

I wasn't sure what to say, but I needn't have worried since Mrs. Butler was quite content to do all the talking – a trait I recognised her daughter seemed to have inherited.

"The thing is, now she's finished school and is waiting for her examination results, it's difficult to keep track of her whereabouts."

"I'm afraid I can't help you there, Mrs. Butler, I haven't spoken to Kelly since well before the play."

"Oh I know that. I wasn't suggesting... Well you see, she's become involved with some people." She bent her head closer to mine, lowering her voice. "We can't find out much about them but there's a group of I think about eight or more and I'm terribly afraid they're some sort of religious fanatics. Some of them are quite a bit older than my daughter, and from what I've heard they meet up in one another's houses. She refuses to tell me where. We've tried following her and are even considering hiring a private detective. That sounds dramatic, doesn't it? Quite frankly we're worried sick that she will go missing again."

"I do sympathise, Mrs. Butler; Kelly is certainly a strong-willed girl, but I still don't quite see how I can help."

34

"Mr. Kendall. Peter. You have obviously inspired my daughter and had a great influence over her. Did you know that she has now applied to several universities in connection with Theatre and Film studies? Well, I know there's a lot of competition in anything to do with acting, but before she met you she was all fired up about going to Art College – I mean, that would certainly be a waste of time."

"Oh I don't think that has much to do with me. Besides, from what I've seen of Kelly's work she has some talent. Art students often go on to enjoy very rewarding and successful careers…"

"You're too modest," she broke in, ignoring the second part of my reply. "All I'm asking is that if you do see her at anytime, perhaps you could have a little chat. She might tell you something about these people. I really would be most grateful."

She patted my hand and stood up, pulling the strap of her bag onto her shoulder. I noticed for the first time since she'd arrived how tired and drawn she looked underneath her immaculate make-up, and I didn't have the heart to destroy the hopeful smile. She gave me a card embossed with her name and mobile number then left. I pushed the card among the bundle of old receipts in the back of my wallet, sure that I would never have occasion to use it. I replaced my wallet in my jacket pocket, thinking all the while of Kelly and feeling the slightest tinge of regret that it was unlikely I would ever see her again, regardless of her mother's belief. It was then as I stepped out into the damp night air that I literally walked straight into her.

Chapter Four

From a kneeling position I sat back on my heels inspecting the clear carpet. I had turned the chairs upright, collected the rubbish and replaced things in their rightful positions. All looked reasonably normal in my lounge again apart from small scraps of paper and muddy marks on the carpet and, of course, the hated green paint daubed on the wall and splashed here and there. I noticed that the weak Autumnal sun had dried the raindrops on my window pane outside during the course of the morning, and now tiny flecks of light, like sparks, danced before my eyes – sunlight reflected off dust particles, I supposed. My skin suddenly prickled uncomfortably at the base of my neck and my spine tingled, raising the fine hairs on my forearms with goose-bumps. There was a bittersweet taste in my mouth, a smell of something familiar yet unreachable on the edge of my memory, and I had an almost urgent desire to listen to Music: Beethoven or Mozart. I stood up, intending to fetch the dustpan and brush from the kitchen, with some dusters, but I felt light-headed and dazed. I managed only a few steps, thudding down on the sofa. The effort this cost reminded me of the time, as a child, when I'd tried to walk under water on the floor of the swimming pool at school. I removed my spectacles, leaned back and closed my eyes, rubbing my temples. I wanted to concentrate, clear my mind of this awful feeling of dread, so I began to count in multiples of seven.

Whispers?
He has to come of his own accord.
He needs to stay with the point in time he was visiting...
His colour is bright. His instincts are strong.
Help him! He's beginning to think in words now instead of

linear vision.
Let it go, please, please let it go…

The front door bell rang and Jem rattled the letterbox, calling through to let me know that he and Eva had returned from shopping. I got up, banishing such peculiar thoughts, and took the rubbish sack with me to put in the wheely bin at the front of the house. I felt drained; my skin was clammy, and my head ached a little. I decided I would finish cleaning and maybe start re-painting after lunch. My stomach rumbled as if on cue. Perhaps some turpentine would clean the splashes of green from the carpet, but the suite would eventually have to be replaced.

Eva's cheese and ham salad baguettes were very welcome, and we talked about the best place to find replacement furniture and how long it would take before the insurance company would pay up on my car. I would have to fund the house repairs from my own pocket, since I'd discovered my home insurance to be inadequate. I offered to help Eva with the dishes but she would have none of that so I excused myself and went back to my own house to work. I declined Jem's offer to come and give me a hand, explaining that there really wasn't much more to do. I'd be out from under their feet before nightfall.

I decided against brushing the floor in favour of using the vacuum cleaner and equipped myself with dusters and furniture polish before hauling the machine out from the cupboard under the stairs. Then I stood for some moments considering whether I should dust and polish first or vacuum. I usually did this when I began housework. I suppose it was a form of procrastination, yet to me it was like trying to solve the age-old riddle of which came first, the chicken or the egg. Vacuuming inevitably stirred up dust, yet polishing meant less dust to vacuum As usual I decided to vacuum first and the low hum of the motor, as I worked my way around the carpet, together with the rhythmic movement required of me, lulled me back into a trance of remembering. Hardly aware of what I was doing I finished cleaning the lounge then continued into the hall, up the stairs and into the bedroom. I was thinking, once again, of the night I had left the burger bar and collided with Kelly, almost knocking her off her feet.

I had lunged forward to catch her by her arms before she could fall and my forehead came into contact with hers, my glasses hitting her sharply across the bridge of her nose. She let out a little yelp of pain, hands flying to her face to check for damage. Fortunately I hadn't really hurt her but I let go, apologising profusely.

"You were with my mother!" She hissed the accusation.

"So where were you then, spying?"

The collision had briefly stunned me but I had no reason to be defensive for it would seem that Kelly had the advantage, being quite aware of my whereabouts while I had in all innocence been completely ignorant of her presence.

"She's always on my case and besides, she and Dad haven't been getting on lately. Now I know why. How long has this been going on?"

"Don't be childish, Kelly," I said mildly. "Your Mother's worried about you. Why don't you try communicating with her a bit more often and put her mind at rest?"

She hung her head, biting her lip, hands thrust deep in her coat pockets.

"It's no good. I'm never going to do it…" she muttered.

I put a hand on her shoulder, "Come on I'll buy you a coffee."

She brightened visibly. "Why don't you come home with me and I'll make you some? It's not far from here and I'm sure my father would like to meet you now that you know my mother."

I shrugged my agreement and fell into step beside her. What was the point of arguing? Maybe I could help Maureen a little after all and I was secretly, just a fraction you understand, pleased to see the girl again. I studied her by the light of the shop windows and street lamps as she chatted on about her plans for the future, her sudden decision to put her desire to paint on the backburner and study at university instead. She hadn't changed very much. She was still quite beautiful, although this was the first time I had really allowed myself to acknowledge the fact and that I, Peter Kendall, was attracted to this lively young woman.

Kelly made no move to take me to meet her father when we arrived at her house. Instead she led the way to the spacious, brightly lit kitchen and proceeded to make the drinks. It was as she spooned freshly ground coffee into a cafetière and set two mugs onto the counter that I asked about her mysterious disappearance. She continued working in silence for a moment, pouring the hot water into the cafetière and stirring, then, without looking up or even acknowledging my question, declared that her parents had no right to interfere with her private affairs or to try to dictate who she could or could not see. I told her that, on the contrary, part of being an adult involved behaving responsibly and that she should have the courtesy to abide by their rules while living in their house. She thrust the plunger down into the glass coffee jug so hard I thought the hot liquid inside would spill out onto the counter.

"I knew you'd take their side. You aren't my teacher now, you know." Her voice had a dangerous edge.

"I never was your teacher, Kelly," I sighed wearily, "I teach primary school."

"Well, just exactly what *are* you to me then?" she challenged defiantly. "You didn't even bother coming to the play. In fact, I haven't seen you since the evening I asked for your friendship, so I guess that put me in my place. You distrusted me so much you went to the trouble of actually avoiding me…"

"It had nothing to do with you." I smothered the guilty memory of my phone call to April Harper that evening. "The world doesn't revolve around you," I spoke gently, half smiling to lighten the mild rebuke. "I had a few things to sort out in my personal life, family matters to attend to."

"So, where does that leave us now? I don't like being ignored or rejected," the petulance could have been construed as childish but the look she gave me was certainly all adult.

Once again I found myself noticing that she was an attractive and interesting young woman. I didn't want the flattery of a crush – I wanted to get to know her better and for her to accept me for who I really was but I needed to take things slowly.

"Let's try again. When you need someone to talk to I'll try to fit you in."

I grinned wolfishly and she finally smiled in return.

"Are you going to take me out on a date then?"

"Don't push your luck!"

"Well how will I get to see you again? I don't mean to be forward, but I can hardly go back to primary school!"

"Why don't you join the Amateur Dramatics Society? You have a while before you need to be in Manchester, don't you? You'll meet a few new faces and one or two familiar ones from *Dream* and guess what my job is…?"

She hesitated, her eyes troubled. I reached forward and took her two hands, holding them loosely in my own. "Whatever happens, we'll always be friends, Okay? As to how far this friendship develops, well let's just wait and see."

So Kelly signed up for Amateur Dramatics and I saw her almost every week as a result. Neither April nor any of my other friends and colleagues ever commented on the friendship – Kelly was no longer at school – but I still held back, restricting our excursions together to the odd theatre trip or an occasional cup of coffee in town. I discouraged any more frequent contact than that. Fortunately, Kelly seemed to accept this for the time being and respect my wishes.

She informed her parents that she was taking a 'gap year'. They were by now settling into their new home in Manchester, and as

Kelly got on well with her aunt with whom she now lived, they had few complaints, although I understood they drove back as often as once or twice a month to see their daughter. They were aware of our friendship but made no protests and I think this was largely because they were relieved to see their daughter a little less rebellious and more accepting of their concerns for her future; she had settled down – I seemed to be a calming influence!

Then Kelly got a weekend and evening job in the large Tesco store on the outskirts of town and began to miss rehearsals for the latest theatre project. This wasn't a problem in itself until I gave Marcia Hills the lead role which Kelly had obviously set her heart on. April, of course, supported my decision though Kelly complained bitterly and vociferously. I attempted to reason with her, explaining that Marcia had been attending evening practises while Kelly hadn't and that I felt she deserved a chance. After all, Marcia had relinquished the role of Hermia in the school production. Kelly disagreed and unreasonably accused me of favouritism, insisting Marcia was my 'little pet', testing my patience to its limits and to some extent undermining my authority with the other dramatists.

To add to the pressure I was behind with my paperwork at school, due to the amount of time I was putting in on extra-curricular activities and fixing up my recently acquired new home. The pleasure of what I saw as a new start for me was dampened a little by a recent telephone call from my sister to say that she and her husband were separating. She'd had bereavement counselling and the couple had tried for another child, but in the end the agony of their loss had a corrosive effect on their relationship; I intuitively knew their marriage wasn't going to make it.

However, that aside, I made allowances for Kelly's jealousy, putting it down to disappointment. Our friendship had matured beyond the 'crush' stage and we generally had a lot in common and got on well together, so I continued to see her every now and then away from the Society. One Saturday evening late in November, we were coming out of The Alberry theatre in London, having enjoyed an excellent production of Chekov's *The Cherry Orchard*, when we met Grace on the arm of a huge, blonde, broad-shouldered chap. I wondered briefly if he had been the interloper on our failed relationship as we shook hands like old friends. After a brief exchange of pleasantries, Grace leaned forward as if to kiss my cheek in farewell and whispered in my ear.

"Rather young, isn't she? I expected you to be with someone a little more sophisticated."

I didn't reply and we parted company, Kelly completely oblivious of what my ex-girlfriend had implied, or the uncomfortable confusion of feelings it had stirred within me. There was little chance for conversation as we hurried to catch our train anyway, but Grace's remark niggled at me, although I didn't know why and I was moody as a result.

As our train left Victoria Station with us safely on board, Kelly began again to complain about Marcia's most recent mistakes during rehearsal, explaining how she should have played the part. I said nothing, staring gloomily out of the black window at the house lights now swimming past as we sped into the night.

"You aren't even listening to me, are you?" Kelly demanded, as the train eventually slowed down for our stop. We pushed our tickets through the slots in the turnstiles and made our way out of the station before I answered. It had given me time to curb my growing annoyance and allowed me to speak calmly but firmly.

"I'm not going to discuss this anymore, Kelly. I've made my decision. There'll be other parts when you will have time to practise but for now Marcia is the better actress."

We walked to her aunt's house in silence, and she didn't even wait for the usual peck on the cheek before closing the door on me. *That suited me fine*, I thought, but I didn't sleep well that night, tossing and turning, as first I wondered whether I'd been too harsh and then feeling cross that Kelly should question my judgment.

The next time we met at the Society, Kelly was doing her best to help and encourage Marcia. She behaved and talked to me as if nothing had happened, even making the odd joke, but I only spoke to her when absolutely necessary. Over the next few weeks I continuously brushed away her attempts at reconciling our differences and treated her with polite formality. I could tell this hurt her but I couldn't help myself and to be fair I was stressed, as I have said, about other things going on in my life.

My mother telephoned me one evening to discuss my sister's impending Decree Nisi. All the acrimonious complaints about my father and the problems caused by my parents' divorce, which had been buried beneath a cloak of sympathy for little Charlie's funeral, now surfaced. After some twenty minutes of being verbally dumped on without a chance of halting the tirade, I exploded in exasperation, telling her angrily that I didn't want to know anymore and slamming the telephone receiver down in its cradle.

Sleepless nights were becoming the norm, and when I did manage to drift off for a few hours, I was having disturbing dreams which I couldn't quite remember upon waking, only that they involved my sister's baby, a stunning girl and some sort of music. I was becoming increasingly tired and frustrated. At school I'd been booked onto courses to improve my Information Technology skills and at about the same time was appointed English co-ordinator when another teacher resigned, so was worrying how I would cope with the extra workload. To add insult to injury, the new books and resources I applied for, which would benefit both English and Drama in the school, were refused due to lack of funds. I felt whichever way I turned and whatever I tried to do, I was constrained and hampered by obstacles.

One Saturday afternoon, almost two months after the meeting with Grace, I was sitting in my lounge, marking compositions that had been set for homework, when I heard the letterbox flap. I went into the hall and picked up a folded sheet of paper from the doormat and this was Kelly's note. I read it through then screwed it up, tossing it into the wastepaper basket in the lounge. I knew I was giving precedence to my own immaturity but had absolutely no compunction to back down and perhaps begin arguing with her again. However, the final line kept repeating in my mind like hiccups on a scratched vinyl record – she'd mentioned prayer as a last resort to sorting things out. Was she again becoming involved with the sinister religious group that her mother had worried about?

Kelly had never spoken to me of her 'friends' and the idea somehow bothered me. Therefore, instead of going to make myself a mug of coffee in the kitchen as I'd intended, I paused on reaching the hallway and opened the front door. I immediately came face to face with Kelly who was standing on the door step, patiently waiting.

"You can come inside on one condition. I want to know about the time you went missing."

She followed me silently into the lounge, but neither of us sat down. The very air of the room was at once heavy and oppressive, as though we'd somehow reverted in those few seconds to the unequal student/teacher relationship. Kelly broke the silence.

"You want to know?"

"Where did you go?"

"I stayed with friends."

"Who are these friends?"

"They're students of philosophy."

"Students? From where?"

"They live in Faversham."

"Where did you meet them?"

"We arranged to meet in The Red Lion after I'd finished up at school. Then I went home with them."

That was not what I'd meant and she knew it. I stared at her hard. She stared back. This conversation was getting me nowhere. On impulse I pulled her to me and kissed her passionately. I felt the first tension of resistance gradually relax from her body as she melted into my embrace. Then I abruptly released her, turned and walked out of the room. She quietly followed me into the kitchen and I could feel her eyes on my back as I filled the kettle.

"Peter?"

"Who are these people, Kelly?" I kept my back to her.

"Is that all you're interested in?"

"Yes, for the time being."

"Just who do you think you are?" she exploded, "James Bond, the real OO7? Well, you can go to hell!" She slammed out of the house.

I took my coffee back into the lounge, set it on the table and rummaged through the wastepaper bin until I found her note. I sat on the edge of my chair, sipping my drink and smoothing the crumpled paper across my knee with my free hand as I re-read the words. Then I took down my volume of Shakespeare's plays and pressed the sheet between the pages of *A Midsummer Night's Dream* and that is where it remained until I was clearing up after the burglary all these years later.

As for Kelly, she returned five minutes later. Amused, I watched from my window as she crossed the street on her way back to me, and I opened the door as she was about to knock.

"I didn't mean that," she said, looking at me steadily. Then, "I'll take you to meet them."

Chapter Five

There was that feeling again, the smell and taste too, and this time accompanied by a humming in my ears. I sat down abruptly, glad that I'd finished the cleaning. Perhaps I was coming down with a virus. It was dusk now and I ought to switch on the light and pull the curtains but the miniscule sparks again tumbled around before my face until my vision blurred so that I closed my eyes. A little rest might help – a nap even.

So near, so near…

The video tape of my memories immediately recommenced playing in my mind.

Kelly had arrived back at my house mid-morning on the following day. She told me that she had arranged to meet some of her friends for lunch in a public bar in Faversham and that they knew to expect a guest. I had attempted unsuccessfully to discover something about Kelly's friends during the short drive to our destination, and was still trying as I parked the car and while we walked for the few minutes it took to reach 'The Leading Light' public house. All she would say was that she had become acquainted with them during the meetings of a discussion group, organised by one of the local churches, during Lent. Perhaps due to Maureen Butler's concerns, my visualisation of them therefore swung between serious, middle-aged bible-bashing cult fanatics and colourful, cannabis-stoned hippies. What I was not prepared for, as we entered the warm smoky atmosphere of the pub, was the agreeable humorous smile of the elderly gentleman who rose to greet us and the affectionate hug afforded Kelly by his equally charming wife.

Kelly introduced the couple as Frank and Pauline Rowell. Frank immediately handed us menu cards and asked what I'd like to drink, before making his way to the bar. Pauline smiled encouragingly and asked how long I'd known Kelly and what I did for a living. I felt as if I'd come to meet Kelly's grandparents and wondered how I could broach the awkward subject concerning their involvement with her. I needn't have worried. As soon as we were settled with our drinks and had ordered our meals, Frank began to explain how they'd met.

The Rowells were both retired lecturers, having previously worked at the University of Kent. They now enjoyed spending their leisure time gardening and meeting up with friends and, in particular, continuing their studies of the various aspects of philosophy and religion they'd previously pursued for work. He assured me that they were always interested in other people's views and he told me they attended courses and lectures whenever they had the opportunity. They had especially enjoyed the discussion group where they first came into contact with Kelly. The question put forward for debate had been the old one of predestination versus freedom of choice and it had been refreshing, he added, to find a young person with such an open and enquiring mind as Kelly. He digressed slightly then, asking how I felt now that all schools were obliged to teach something about other religions rather than just Christianity. He listened, nodding sympathetically as I expressed my opinion that it would help fight prejudice and encourage tolerance of other people's cultures and beliefs, now that we were becoming a much more integrated society.

By the time we had finished our meals and were preparing to part, I realised I had spent much of the time talking about myself, rather than discovering all about Kelly's friends, but it no longer seemed so important. As to the other folk with whom they apparently met on a regular basis, that was really none of my business.

However, I did ask about Kelly's stay with them and was rewarded with such a sharp glare from her that I expected a kick under the table to accompany it but the Rowells didn't seem to mind in the least. Pauline mildly explained that their young friend had asked if she could use their home as a retreat for a few days, while she sorted out some personal problems, and they had agreed. It was as simple as that. At eighteen, Kelly was not obliged to inform her parents of her whereabouts so I let the matter drop.

My doorbell rang, bringing me back to the present with a jolt. Jem had come to fetch me for supper. Once I'd eaten, Eva handed me my freshly laundered and ironed clothes, waving away my thanks. Then she gave me a little plastic tub containing some lose change and Kelly's letter, apologising that she'd forgotten about emptying the contents of my pockets. I took the letter from the tub, sighing; I'd all but forgotten the cause of all my reminiscing but was glad to see the blue envelope again and determined to keep it safely in my hand until I could examine its content. Eva noticed my slight obsession with the letter but asked no questions, merely patting my arm kindly and telling me to go home and read it.

My dearest Peter,

I am writing in the hope that you will help me, as I have nobody else to whom I can turn. Please forgive me, I have no choice but to write; I know how hard it must have been for you to rebuild your life when I left.

I hope you will believe me when I tell you that I didn't want to leave you but I chose what I thought to be the best solution for both of us. Please try not to be angry or resentful. If you will give me the opportunity I will explain everything to you. I am not able to make any promises as to when I can come but I will try to visit you soon.

Kelly.

Not even signed with love, I noted. I put the letter back into its envelope and balanced it on top of the book of Shakespeare's plays. Then, agitated, I began to pace. I knew I should be thinking of preparing for school on Monday but I decided I needed to get out and exercise a little, use up some of the adrenaline surge that had responded to the ancient need within me for fight or flight. I suddenly craved fresh air. I grabbed a jacket and left the house, slamming the door shut behind me, no longer preoccupied with security for what good had it done me? My mind was a whirl. I had expected more from the letter but it did at least promise some sort of resolution to the questions surrounding Kelly's disappearance. When would those answers come, though?

My feet took me across town, out towards a neighbouring village and beyond, along country lanes and finally to the sea wall, about seven miles in all, although I didn't notice the distance.

It was quite dark as I eventually reached my destination, crunching my way along the shingle, but my eyes had become accustomed to the intermittent moonlight bathed in cloud. The tide was out but I could hear the restless roll of the waves and an icy breeze numbed my face and hurt my ears. I stopped for a moment, bending to feel around the ground about my feet and then I picked up a small, flat pebble and rubbed it between my finger and thumb, absent-mindedly checking the smooth surface for any defects. It had been a habit adopted by Kelly and myself in the early days of our courtship. She told me she loved me for the first time on this very beach and had stooped down to pick up a pebble, after I'd replied that I felt the same. She had said that every time we came to this spot we must find a stone to carry home to remind us of the day so that we would never take our love for granted. Each pebble must, she had always insisted, be complete; it could be worn but not broken. She had kept the pebbles in a large, old fashioned sweet jar, which over time became quite decorative with all the different colours, shapes and sizes. I still had that jar of pebbles in the bathroom at my house and it was barely a third of the way to being full. Our time together as lovers had not covered such a lengthy span, I realised with regret.

My thoughts flew back over the years once more as I walked the length of the beach, shoulders hunched against the chill.

It had taken a little over a year for our relationship to evolve from our first encounter at Greenacres, becoming friends, and finally admitting love. However, as much as I wanted to be with her, I had been keen for Kelly to pursue her career and 'find herself' as she had once put it, so I encouraged her to go to university. She spent three years living occasionally with her parents and often on campus, engrossed in Film and Theatre studies, yet writing every couple of days to me and telephoning each weekend. I visited whenever I could and spent time with the Butlers, getting to know them in my new guise as prospective son-in-law.

Our wedding finally took place in a little church near the university, some four months after Kelly's graduation. Maureen was a little disappointed that we had opted for a quiet, simple ceremony but nevertheless seemed to enjoy her role as mother of the bride. I could now do no wrong in either of Kelly's parents' eyes. The few members of my own family did not attend for various reasons but sent their best wishes and I did not allow their absence to detract from the day.

Kelly and I decided to wait before trying for children and once we had settled into married life back in Kent she began applying for jobs in earnest. Then, seven months later she was gone, as if our life together had never existed. There had been no argument, no difference in the routine of our life; I just returned home from school one day to find her missing.

At first I had thought she would be out shopping, visiting friends or on some other errand, although it was unusual for her not to leave a note. I was a little disappointed as I'd had an interesting conversation at school with a woman from a visiting drama team, who'd spent the day leading workshops for pupils in year 5. The team went from school to school performing and teaching and the woman had informed me that they were looking for a new recruit, a young woman, as one of their members had recently announced that she was pregnant. It probably wasn't the sort of glamorous job Kelly had envisaged embarking on at the beginning of her career but it would be a start, something to keep her occupied. I'd been rehearsing persuasive arguments all the way home only to find an empty house but never mind, it could wait. I made myself a sandwich then set to work planning lessons for the week ahead. However, as time passed I became a little anxious and by late evening, uneasiness had developed into dread.

I remember that night so well, contacting her parents, our friends, anyone I could think of but nobody had any idea where she might be. I didn't go to bed, worrying through the long, slow hours, hoping for her return, willing the telephone to ring, waiting for her to somehow break the silence and loneliness of the empty house. I wandered aimlessly from room to room, noting traces of her existence everywhere; a book lay open on the arm of the sofa, an unwashed coffee cup stood near the sink and in our bedroom the door of the closet hung slightly ajar (a broken latch awaiting my DIY talents being the cause), revealing her clothes hung neatly in line, dresses, blouses, skirts and trouser suits. Little pots of creams and lotions were carefully arranged near her hairbrush on the dressing table. I called her name, half expecting her to reply from another room in the house but of course she didn't. I was completely and utterly alone, more alone than I had ever felt in my entire life.

I contacted the police and eventually a missing person report was filed, but a few days later I received a call from an officer informing me that the young woman in question had been in contact and they were satisfied that no crime had been committed. However, although they sympathised with me and had advised her to get in touch, they were unable to reveal to me her whereabouts. I was bewildered, frustrated and finally angry as time went on and she failed to reappear.

I'd managed to trace the Rowells through the local church but they had no answers to give. I spoke to them on the telephone and they invited me to their home for a meal and to talk, but I politely declined. I knew Kelly kept in contact with them and her other friends but she had gradually talked less frequently about the meetings and conversations they had shared and I believed she'd simply lost interest. When I'd explained the reason for my call they appeared as mystified by Kelly's disappearance as I was, and I had no reason to believe they would deceive me.

Eventually, as weeks merged into months and then years, feelings of frustration gave way to hurt and despair. After a while I even took Brian Cooke's advice and saw a counsellor.

"Oh Kelly, where are you?"

The question, so often repeated in the past, was now snatched from my lips by the mournful wind and carried out to sea. I dropped the little pebble into my pocket and hugged my coat closer to me, coughing slightly as the bitter, briny air assaulted my lungs. Reluctantly I left the beach, weary after my exertion but now empty of the negative feelings that had been conjured up by the exasperating letter. I saw a small light flickering on the lane ahead, which I soon discovered to be the torchlight of a fellow pedestrian coming towards me. Some few metres away a woman called out and hurried forward and I was surprised to come face to face with Kelly's mother.

"Maureen, what on earth are you doing here?"

"I came to find you. The car's parked just along the road."

I followed her, glad of the warmth and comfort of the Mercedes. Maureen fetched a thermos flask from the boot and poured coffee, giving me some before settling into the driver seat to enjoy her own, the thermos safely stowed back in the rear of the car.

"You heard from Kelly." She sipped her drink and watched as I drank mine, gratefully warming my hands round the cup.

"I had a letter but it didn't tell me anything. I was going to call."

"I had phone calls but nobody spoke, there was just a pause before the receiver was replaced. It happened three times yesterday. I dialled 1471 for the number but it had been withheld, so I decided to drive over to see if you'd heard anything. Your neighbours explained about the break-in and said that they believed you'd had a letter. I thought you might be here."

"I'll show you the letter if you like. It's truly infuriating – explains nothing! Where did you get this wonderful coffee?"

"Well, it was a long drive and I thought I'd stop for a break along the way but never got round to it." She smiled. "No need to show me the letter, Peter. I'm just glad I found you and can give you a ride home." She handed me her cup and started the engine.

At the time it didn't occur to me how odd it was that she should drive all this way, then not even wish to inspect her daughter's letter. Neither did we talk anymore about where Kelly might be, or when we might find her, after our initial greeting. I enjoyed the remainder of the coffee, relishing the warmth of the car's interior while Maureen drove in silence, concentrating on the road ahead.

I really did appreciate the lift; it would have been a long walk back and I was now quite exhausted and said as much when we arrived at my house. I offered my mother-in-law a room for the night but she gracefully declined.

"I'll stay over at the travellers' accommodation near Bobbing and start back at the crack of dawn. I know you'll get in touch as soon as you know anything. Goodnight, Peter. Try to get some sleep."

I watched her drive away, suddenly realising that it was the first time we'd spoken in over four years, not because of any dispute, just a simple, unspoken acknowledgment that it was too painful for either of us to be constantly reminded of Kelly's absence from our lives. Her admonition to rest was really unnecessary. My body was so heavy when I climbed the stairs that I felt quite drunk and quickly fell naked into bed, too tired even to bother with pyjamas. As I drifted into sleep I was aware of a pleasant sensation of weightlessness and I began to dream vividly.

I felt myself floating and opened my eyes to find a milky-white substance all about me. I marvelled at the texture; it was opaque, too soft and smooth to be solid, yet without the patchiness and damp of mist or fog. The substance was continuous and completely enveloped me, yet peculiarly I was aware that it would be quite possible to ignore it, if I chose to, and see the world around me quite as clearly as if the substance was not there. I allowed myself to melt into the silkiness and gradually became conscious that I was standing with a group of people in a cobbled yard. I was holding a beautiful black cat, which amused me because I am generally allergic to the fine hairs of animals in ordinary everyday life and couldn't enjoy petting them without the warning itch of my nostrils, followed later by severe breathing difficulties. The cat purred as I stroked her, and I carefully put her down and followed my companions through a tall, narrow wrought iron gate into a gorgeous classical nineteenth century English garden with green lawns stretching as far as one could see. There was an abundance of trees and flowers, butterflies and birds, even the melodious droning of a bumble bee. I saw two pretty little girls, dressed in fancy frocks, hair in long brown ringlets tied with ribbons in bunches on both sides of their heads. They were happily inspecting a sundial. My companions watched with me as the children played, and I commented that they would surely grow into fine young ladies. The man beside me, I didn't look at his face yet felt familiar with him, corrected me saying that actually the children were not human at all but puppies and that they would grow into handsome bitches.

"But that's no dog!" I pointed to the nearest child incredulously and for a split second she turned and looked at me solemnly so that I was immediately sorry for my outburst.

"It's all to do with perception", a woman, that I also seemed to know without looking at her, soothed. "For some lonely or unfulfilled people, pets become their children and are every bit as human to them as we are which means here they appear as human beings."

Then I was enveloped in colour – first red, then green, then blue. I heard numbers chanted and felt at peace. It reminded me of the way I dealt with stress by doing mental arithmetic or counting. Next, I was on a hillside. The same group of people appeared to be with me and I knew them to be my friends. We were about to dig up a metal cash box, which apparently contained something that would be prized by one of our male friends for his birthday. Unfortunately, the woman digging uncovered a trainer as she sliced through the spongy turf with her spade. We all laughed, joking that the chap must have buried a body here. I too had a spade and began to dig near a small, wiry bush but quickly uncovered the other white trainer and a yellow one with a navy stripe that I recognised as belonging to Kelly. I tried to cover the shoes again with crumbly earth without exciting anyone's attention.

Suddenly I was standing with somebody in a small, shallow cave. The floor was man-made with planks of wood and I understood that the 'birthday boy's' coffin lay beneath these boards. I sensed a wooden ramp behind us and water, boats even, although I saw none of these things. I now had only one male companion who pointed out some ancient symbols scratched on the wall of the cave in a corner near the floor. I recognised one but could not think from where. My companion reassured me the symbol had been sent out to everyone 'on the calendar'. This knowledge troubled me and I struggled to understand why. I concentrated hard and immediately found myself in an old church, cathedral or some such gothic building, sitting on a bench in a semi-circle; the seating reminded me of that found in Roman amphitheatres. My companion stood up and left. Unconcerned, I looked over to my right and recognised Kelly's school boyfriend, Tony, who had played Demetrius in *A Midsummer Night's Dream*. I called out a greeting to him. He didn't react, just left his seat and made his way to the area in front of the seating, stopping to speak to someone two seats in front of me. I was certain he had heard me but was deliberately ignoring me and avoiding looking my way. Then he too walked off. I pretended not to care, joining the person he'd spoken to and conversing in a loud, exuberant manner so that Tony would hear me. I thought to myself that I was glad because his refusal to acknowledge my presence obviously meant he was jealous of me and he therefore couldn't be Kelly's present lover. The person I'd engaged in conversation suddenly laughed and looked up. I followed the direction of her gaze and saw millions of stars which seemed to move closer without falling until they were all around us. I realised I was alone and floating again and was soon enveloped once more in the milky substance. I looked down and realised with sudden horror that I could see myself, lying in my bed. I experienced a rush of colours and a spinning sensation and woke with a jolt, covered in sweat.

It took me several seconds to recover and I sat on the edge of my bed, rubbing my face, and thinking about how to note down all the different parts of the strange dream before I forgot them. I reached for the notebook and pen, hesitating half-way. My mouth felt dry and I was still a little shaken so I decided to get a glass of milk before even attempting the task. I pulled on my dressing-gown and groped my way down the stairs, not bothering with the landing light but flicking the switch in the hall-way. I started forward to the kitchen then abruptly stopped. The kitchen light was already on and standing near the window blind, framed by the doorway, stood Kelly, watching me.

I'd thought so often of the time when I would come face to face with Kelly again and the things I would say, but now the moment had arrived I found myself incapable of either movement or word.

"Hello Peter," she paused as if waiting for a response and then suddenly continued in a rush, "I'm sorry I can't stay long, so I need you to listen to me carefully. There isn't much time."

I just stood and stared at her so she took my silence as agreement.

"I want you to find a second-hand bookshop in Canterbury which has a symbol that you recognise above the door. Look on the second floor for the section on histories of different countries around the world and their religions. Somewhere among all the volumes you'll find a small poetry book. It doesn't have a title and the author isn't named but you'll know it's the book I mean because it has a large star and four smaller ones engraved on the front cover. It's old and battered and doesn't look particularly valuable."

"Kelly what, in God's name, are you on about?" I finally interjected. "I haven't seen you in over five years and you suddenly appear and start giving me instructions to find some book!"

"Five years. Has it really been that long? Oh, Peter, I'm so sorry but it's vitally important you do as I ask."

"Kelly," I was becoming impatient and slightly angry now, "Why did you leave me, and where have you been? Was it something I did? I know you weren't happy about being unable to get work straight away, but we could have sorted something out if you'd only talked to me."

"There isn't time for that now. If you still love me, please do as I ask. I'm relying on you. Meet me at Stillbury Church on Sunday week at 5:00 p.m. and bring the book with you. Oh and pay close attention to any dreams you have – they should help."

"Now you're beginning to sound like my therapist," I started forward, impatiently. "You know I still love you, so let's cease this silly nonsense and talk properly."

"No, Peter, don't touch me!" she cried in alarm. Her eyes flashed bright with fear bringing me to an uncertain stop before her, hands dropping to my sides.

"Kelly," I said sadly, "you do know I'd never hurt you, surely?" Our eyes locked for a long minute then I reached for her. She screamed. I shall never forget the sound; it was inhuman, unearthly, and my hand passed right through her as she disintegrated in a blur of darkness. I stood, shaking and alone in the empty kitchen.

Chapter Six

"Peter, I hope you appreciate this session will be expensive, it being Sunday?" Phillip Wells, my therapist, waited for my assent before indicating that I should enter his office. I sat down and watched as he retrieved and rummaged through my file before taking his seat. I don't think he was particularly concerned about taking my hard-earned cash, he was just checking that there would be adequate remuneration for his inconvenience.

"I thought I'd seen the last of you. You've hardly attended a session this year and now this sudden urgency. I'm curious, has something happened?"

"The dreams are back, only now they're more vivid."

"I see. Have you been keeping the dream diary as before?" I nodded and he made a note on his pad. "Perhaps I'll have a look at that at a later date. Has anything traumatic happened to you recently that you think might have triggered the dreams?"

I told him about the break-in at my house and the damage to my car, although I assured him that these occurrences were more of a nuisance than anything else. Then I explained about the positive things going on in my life. Following my successful work as subject leader, I'd been offered the chance at the Deputy Headship at school, and though I wasn't sure I was ready for the responsibility yet, I felt kind of proud to be considered. Young Thomas Jenkins intruded suddenly on my thoughts, closely followed by Caroline Lyman's persistent hints that we ought to get together socially, and I sighed.

Then I thought about Kelly's letter and the way I'd come across the old poem and re-read it, kneeling amid the remnants of my lounge. Wells made copious notes as I talked.

"You'll probably think I'm crazy, but I went for a long walk and ended up near the sea in the dead of night. It was lucky that my mother-in-law turned up to rescue me because I was so tired I might have ended up having a cosy night sleeping on the beach!" I'm not sure whether my attempt at flippancy was for his benefit or my own.

"I think the walk was possibly a very sensible reaction to the stress you've been under. As to the dreams, I take it they're still about your wife? It's hardly surprising all the old wounds have been re-opened after receiving her letter and then seeing your mother-in-law. Now, tell me all that you can remember about the first dream."

***

An unexpected bonus of having no car at the time was that I had to be organised enough to be punctual getting to work and as a result arrived rather earlier than usual on Monday morning. I pushed my way through the double doors leading from the reception area and stopped to admire the poster Caroline had attached to the wall near the hall door. A fat green beanstalk wound its way from the bottom of the paper to the top, like a snake hampered by curly leaves supporting the odd cartoon-like caterpillar. The stalk vanished into a fluffy cloud surrounded by blue sky. At the bottom of the picture a matchstick lad with brown haystack hair, knobbly knees and thin arms protruding from his body, held onto a rope which was secured to a lopsided cow. Bright red letters above these characters proclaimed:

Come and See
If you can be
in Jack and the Beanstalk.
Meet Mr. Kendall here at
3:30 p.m. on Wednesday.

As I beamed at the poster I was aware of the flat-shoed, heavy tread of a man along the corridor behind me. He came to a halt by my side.

"Rather good, isn't it? I helped Miss Lyman pick the winners since you were absent Friday afternoon. I hope you don't mind."

I turned to face my new companion, "And you would be?"

"Sorry, I thought you'd know. I'm the new teacher for Year 5. I don't officially start until next term but I thought I'd come in, check the place out and get to know everybody. Mark Chapman." He took his hand from his trouser pocket and shook my own heartily. He had a good firm handshake and I felt myself warm to him immediately as I briefly took in the straight shoulders and his comfortable, casual clothes: brown slacks and cream shirt, sleeves rolled up to his elbows. His hair was red, thinning slightly on top, and his face was youthfully freckled, complimented by a wide, good-natured smile.

"Ah yes, I'd forgotten. Good to meet you Mark."

"I understand we're the only two male teachers in the school, apart from the Head, so perhaps we can stick together. I must say though, I rather like Caroline. Do you know if she's seeing anyone? Sorry if I seem a bit forward, I'm nervous as hell really." He ran a hand through his hair then stuffed both hands back into his pockets. "Feel like I'm on probation already and I haven't even started teaching yet..."

"Oh, I think Caroline might be persuaded to meet up with you for a drink. Would you like me to arrange it?" I grinned in return.

"Are you joking? Please do. I've a feeling you and I are going to get on like a house on fire, if you'll pardon the expression." He put his hand on my shoulder by way of a friendly gesture as we moved off down the corridor. I glanced at it briefly, then back at his face and he hastily removed it. "Sorry, getting a bit carried away. Well, see you later I expect." He proceeded off down the corridor towards the infants' section of the school. I stood watching, shaking my head in amusement. He'd be back in a minute when he realised

61

his mistake. At that precise moment Caroline emerged from the library.

"See you've met Mark then?" She stood arms folded, head to one side, following the direction of my gaze. "He was a scientist you know, employed at that Research Centre before they closed it down and made him redundant. That's when he decided to take up teaching, about three years ago. He was employed at a private school before he came here." She nodded her approval.

"You seem to know a lot about him."

"Nice bloke – gregarious. By the way we're all meeting up for a drink to officially welcome him at lunchtime. Coming?"

"Of course."

"Good. Oh, and we've decided on next Saturday evening for Pheobe's leaving do. Have you any suggestions where we should go?"

I thought for a moment.

"Doesn't she live in Ospringe? How about Canterbury; there are some nice restaurants and clubs there."

"Kendall, you're an absolute star! Excellent idea." She kissed me on the cheek impulsively. "We can talk to the others at break, while she's going through pupil records with Mark. Then maybe this evening we could drive down on a 'reccy' straight after school, since the staff meeting's cancelled."

"Sorry, no can do. I'm going to see about test driving new cars this afternoon.
It's just a thought, Caz, but why don't you invite Mark instead? He seems a discerning sort of guy. Besides, he likes you."

She darted a suspicious glance at me. "Well, you're in a good mood. I suppose it would make him feel more welcome if we included him. Do you really think he likes me?"

"Know so!" I gave her arm a friendly squeeze. "Go for it." I sauntered off to find Brian.

The excuse about test driving new cars was really only a white lie, as I did fully intend to call the insurance company after school so that I could decide which garages and showrooms it might be worth visiting at the weekend. I also had another appointment with Phillip Wells and after that I wanted to get all my marking and planning up to date and have an early night, if possible.

The appointment with Wells was short and pretty uninformative for my part. I continued to fill him in on my dreams and reached the one where I'd been in the cave tomb when the session time was up. He'd said very little, writing notes much of the time and only pausing to look at me occasionally by way of encouragement. I handed him my dream diary as I got up to leave.

"Thanks for fitting me in yesterday and today – it's really helped. Perhaps you could have a read through my diary before my next appointment. I don't think I need to see you again until the end of next week, if that's okay with you?"

He looked at me in silence for a moment, his expression serious. "I think we should make it this Friday, just until we sort out these nightmares, agreed? I'm glad you seem to be feeling a little better though."

"Well," I took my jacket from his antique hat stand by the door and put it on, "let's just say things are starting to look up a bit. I'll tell you all about it on Friday then. For now I've another appointment, with a pile of marking and a mug of cocoa."

In truth, I was beginning to feel things were indeed sorting themselves out. Sunday night I'd slept deeply and dreamlessly and had felt rested and ready for the following day as a result. My little problem of avoiding Caroline's feminine overtures seemed to be solving itself with the arrival of Mark. Then, of course, the insurance company had made me a rather more generous offer than I'd expected on my car, which they'd promised to confirm in writing before the end of the week. I had been meaning to replace the mini for some time so I was looking forward to driving one or two different models before making my final choice. I'd had my eye on a smart new Toyota for a while now and even if it would mean dipping into my savings to fund the excess, I felt it would be worth it – something to really look forward to. It was good to have so many positive things to ponder that Kelly couldn't impinge on my thoughts too often. Since I'd been talking to my therapist I'd come to the conclusion that the incident in the kitchen had been nothing more than an extension of my nightmares and I anticipated Phillip's sensible explanation, when I came to telling him that episode of my dreams, with some relish.

On the way home I picked up a Chinese takeout and a bottle of wine, having cheerfully decided to treat myself and forego the cocoa. Dusk was falling and the street lights were beginning to come on as I turned the corner onto my road. My foot caught the edge of an uneven part of the pavement and I tripped, almost falling, but I managed to recover my balance quickly. As I looked up towards my house I saw somebody come out of the front door, walk down the short path and out of the gate and turn to stride away in the opposite direction. I immediately recognised him as the tall, thin 'spy'. I yelled in surprise and anger and began to run, but he was too far ahead of me and although he neither turned at my shout nor hastened his gait, I soon lost sight of him in the failing light. I retraced my steps hurriedly, fumbling impatiently for my key and juggling the bag of hot food and bottle of alcohol as I did so. I flicked the switch to the hall light as I stepped through the door, dreading what I might find, and then slowly entered my lounge eyes and mouth wide open in amazement. The room had been completely redecorated, the carpet and sofa replaced with identical newer versions of the old. I left my purchases in the kitchen and hurried round to the Scotts.

Jem and Eva admitted they had seen workmen at the house. They had been surprised but pleased that I'd managed to organise somebody to do the job at such short notice rather than trying to do everything myself. When I told them that I'd done no such thing Jem frowned.

"How did they get your key then? They didn't ask for ours

and I must say I did think it a little strange that you hadn't told us someone was coming."

I thought for a moment. They didn't have my key and the only other person to have one was Kelly. This must have been her doing. I said as much and the Scotts exchanged uneasy looks.

"Don't you think that's a little unlikely after all this time, Lad. I mean, you haven't heard from her in years, have you?" Eva enquired gently.

"Yes I have. She wrote to me. You remember the letter you took from my trousers pocket when you laundered them?"

"Oh. I didn't realise that was from Kelly."

"Yes. I'm sure I showed you. Anyway, you told my mother-in-law that she'd written to me."

These words were met with blank looks and genuine puzzlement. "When was that, dear?"

I chuckled in disbelief, "Yesterday. She came round to see you because I was out on a walk." I looked from one to the other expectantly.

"We haven't seen anyone, Son. We didn't even know you'd gone for a walk."

I was beginning to feel I'd stepped into another of my nightmares. I scratched my head. "Well, don't worry about it. I probably misunderstood what she said. I was very tired when I saw her. Anyway, I'm going to go and get my Chinese food while it's still warm. Sorry to have disturbed you."

"I'm glad your house has been sorted out," Jem called round his front door, as I let myself back into my own home. I put a hand up to him in acknowledgment, although I wasn't so sure I agreed entirely with his sentiments; it was all a little too odd for my liking. I didn't like the idea of strangers in my house without my knowledge or permission and I certainly didn't like the fact that I'd seen the 'spy' stepping out of my front door, looking as if he owned the place. What was Kelly thinking? I went over to my shelves and reached for her letter which I'd left balanced on the book of Shakespeare's plays. It was gone. I searched the rest of the shelves, behind the books, the floor, behind the couch but I could not find it anywhere. Then I remembered what the Scotts had said about not seeing Maureen. My stomach growled hungrily yet I needed to solve this mystery somehow, so before eating I went to the hallway and telephoned the Butlers.

After only three rings Mr. Butler's voice came on the line.

"John? Peter here. I'm sorry to call at this hour but would it be possible for me to have a quick word with Maureen?"

There was a few seconds silence before he replied, his voice low, depressed,
"I'm sorry, Peter. I really have been meaning to call you. I'm afraid Maureen was involved in a motorway accident late Friday night. She's in a coma but they don't think she's going to make it."

Chapter Seven

"Peter, did you hear what I said?" My father-in-law broke the disbelieving pause that followed. Stunned and confused, I mumbled some sort of apology and asked that he let me know if there was anything I could do before replacing the receiver. I sat down heavily on the bottom of my stairs and remained there for some time, head in hands, distraught. Quite apart from the distress about Maureen's serious medical condition, I was completely bewildered, certain that I'd seen her only yesterday evening when apparently she was a couple of hundred miles away, lying in a hospital bed unconscious. Eventually I got up, went back to the telephone and dialled.

"Hi April, what are you up to at the moment?" I was amazed at how steady and normal I managed to keep my voice.

"Hello stranger! It's nice to hear from you after all this time. I was about to stick a ready meal in the microwave but it can wait if you want a chat. How's that play coming along?"

"Don't ask about the play – I haven't even started it. How about putting your food back in the fridge and joining me for a Chinese here? I've got a bottle of wine chilling and could do with some company."

"Are you okay Peter? You sound a bit peculiar."

"I've just had a bit of bad news."

"Alright, I'll be round in five. Do you mind if I bring some work with me? Sorry to be a killjoy but I can't afford to get behind with an OFSTED inspection looming."

I put the food in the oven to keep warm and set the table then went into the lounge to make a start on my own marking. April was a little longer arriving than I'd anticipated, so I was able to push a satisfying two thirds of the exercise books I'd been correcting to one side when I finally heard her at the door.

Over the meal she told me excitedly of her new relationship with an ice-skating instructor; April had 'come out' as a lesbian while we were at college together. It had never been an issue between us but our friendship had caused the occasional rift with her first partner, Suzy, who had studied with us and had been a little suspicious that we felt so comfortable in one another's company. I believe this was one of the contributing factors to the failure of the relationship, even though April never admitted as much in so many words.

As we finished the meal, April went on to inform me that Amdram, the local Amateur Dramatics Society, had temporarily stopped meeting shortly after I had given up attending. My excuse had been that I wanted to concentrate on my writing for a while and perhaps come up with a new play. I shook my head, staring at the table and refusing to apologise or excuse myself. I didn't feel guilty because I knew they had been relying on me too much and were stuck in a rut. If they were to survive they needed fresh blood and new ideas. I decided it was time to change the subject, so I told her some of my news, about the burglary, the car and finally Maureen's accident. April had brought another bottle of wine with her so I emptied the remainder of my Muscadet into her glass and proceeded to open the second bottle.

"You know, this would really go better with seafood. You'll probably find mine a bit sweeter. My friend," she lifted her glass, "I am beginning to feel rather nice and relaxed now and not at all in the mood for marking."

"Sorry. Do you want me to put this back on ice for another day?"

"Certainly not, the marking will have to wait."

"I was rather hoping you'd say that," I filled my own glass and took a gulp, "because I would like your opinion on something. April, apart from our difference of opinion about the Society, do I seem normal to you? I mean, do you think I should be worried about my mental state of health?"

"Well, chum, you've always seemed a little odd to us ordinary mortals but that's part of your charm." April giggled into her drink until she noticed I wasn't sharing the joke. She put her glass down carefully, studying me closely. "You're serious, aren't you?"

"Deadly serious," I assured her, "and when I've finished telling you everything I want you to give me an honest reply."

I told her I'd started having extremely vivid dreams, which concerned me enough to seek help from my old counsellor. Then I explained about Kelly's letter and how I had gone for a long walk to try to sort out my feelings about possibly seeing her again. She listened patiently and it was a relief not to have someone scribbling away as I talked, but to know that I had her full attention as a friend. I told her about meeting Maureen Butler and our conversation when she gave me a lift home. Then, watching her face cautiously, afraid almost to meet her eye, I explained that this had occurred apparently after my mother-in-law had been in the accident. I waited for April's response.

"Do you think perhaps you fell asleep and imagined the walk because you were upset?" she suggested at last.

I went to the hall and brought back my jacket, searching in the pocket for the pebble which I put on the table in front of her. "I picked that up off the beach."

"Yes but you could have dreamed the part about your mother-in-law when you got back. I mean, you were obviously quite upset and disturbed by the letter, the break-in and everything and you always got on well with Kelly's mum."

69

I hung my jacket on the back of the chair I'd been sitting on and raked distractedly at my hair. "You're right. The pebble doesn't really prove anything does it?"

"Peter, don't be so hard on yourself, you've been through a lot and I don't think you're losing your marbles. After all, you've had the sense to seek help." She stretched and yawned. "There's obviously something else bothering you so why don't you let me make us some coffee and we'll sit in your front room, where the chairs aren't so hard."

"Coffee? That's it!" I bounded across the kitchen, flinging open a cupboard door so hard the metal handle cracked against the panelling next to it. I took down two small stainless steel coffee cups. "These are the cups we drank from when we got back to the car. She gave me her empty cup to hold so she could drive, while I finished my drink. When I got indoors, after waving her off, I realised I still had them both."

April looked a little sceptical. "You're sure they aren't the cups to your own thermos?"

"Oh come on, April. Even if I do have a flask, and I'm fairly sure I don't, it's probably a cheap one with plastic cups. These classy items definitely belong to Maureen Butler. I didn't dream our meeting." I felt myself flush with triumph and I couldn't keep from smiling, relieved beyond belief that I wasn't losing my mind after all.

"In that case, there must be a rational explanation. I'll stack the plates. You make the coffee." April stood up and started clearing the table. "Then you can show me this letter Kelly sent."

"I can't, it's gone. That's another odd thing. When I got home today my lounge had been completely redecorated, re-furnished and re-carpeted. It must have been something to do with Kelly because nobody else has a key apart from the Scotts and they were as bemused as I was."

We abandoned the idea of coffee and took our wine into the

front room and sat down, April looking all around at the freshly painted walls.

"I also saw this bloke coming out of my front door as I walked up the road tonight but I wasn't quick enough to catch up with him. He looked a lot like a man I thought I saw watching the house one night when I had a dream about Kelly being in the room."

"Don't you think you ought to inform the police?"

"And tell them what – that somebody kindly sorted out my lounge free of charge without even having to break in? They'd think I was barmy and you couldn't blame them, I was beginning to think so myself."

April's expression suddenly changed. "Peter, just suppose it wasn't a dream. What if Kelly really was with you?"

"But she vanished, April. People don't just vanish into thin air!" I grimaced as I suddenly remembered the night in the kitchen when I'd thought I'd been talking to her and she had disintegrated.

"What is it?"

When I told her what had happened I expected at best for her to patronise me, but instead she started talking about premonitions and scientific research into telepathy, and the like, suggesting that perhaps I was seeing Kelly because I intuited that she was in trouble.

"Mind you, it doesn't completely explain everything," she finished at last and before I could completely take in all that she'd been saying or make any comment she added, "Quite frankly, Peter, I think there's only one thing to do. We have to go and find this book she was talking about."

Chapter Eight

There was a time I would have scoffed at April's suggestions but my recent experiences left me uncertain and I was at least willing to find out more about psychic phenomena. With this in mind, I went straight up to the staffroom at break time the next day hoping to locate Chapman. I discovered him sitting alone, looking through the pile of magazines, papers and information sheets strewn across the coffee table, which advertised various teaching posts and vacancies for classroom assistants in Kent and the surrounding region. I struck up a conversation, casually asking how he was enjoying being in school during the winding down period leading to the end of term. I sat down as he shrugged and told me he was looking forward to starting his job in earnest. Then he thanked me for giving him the opportunity to ask Caroline out and confided they were having dinner that evening. Other members of staff began to filter into the staffroom and I decided if I was going to ask his opinion as a scientist on parapsychology and the paranormal, it would have to be now – I didn't want a big audience or too many participants in the conversation.

"Mark, what do you think of such things as telepathy and premonitions?" I asked quickly before I had chance to change my mind.

He helped himself to a biscuit from a tin provided by one of the teachers, who was celebrating a birthday – usually we had cakes. He promptly dunked the bourbon biscuit in his coffee before replying.

"Well, it's quite a controversial area of research," he said between mouthfuls.

"I tend to keep an open mind. There are scientists who accept mind control as a given and are attempting to establish a link with quantum theory," he grinned without meeting my eye and I wondered whether he was pulling my leg. Still, I waited silently as he chewed on another biscuit thoughtfully. "Some hypothesise that man's still evolving and thought transference, telekinesis and presentiment are all examples of human development. Then, of course, psychologists are looking at the effect on the mind of the mere belief in such phenomena and possible connections between psychosis and other mental disorders. On the other hand, since Victorian times there have been scientists willing to risk their reputations on research into the paranormal – chap called Wallis – associate of Darwin being a prime example."

"I wouldn't have thought you'd be interested in such mumbo jumbo." Caroline joined us, uninvited. Neither of us were sure to whom she had addressed her remark.

"Actually, some of the papers that appear in the science journals from time to time are truly quite fascinating," Mark protested mildly. "Would you like me to look some out for you, Peter?"

"Oh, surely you aren't thinking of including some sort of supernatural element in the next play you're writing." Caroline laughed and I shifted in my seat uncomfortably.

However, I needn't have worried about trying to explain myself for Chapman intervened. "Come now, Caroline. If the Master can use such tools, why can't our friend? Think of the witches in Macbeth and the ghost of Hamlet's father."

There was a momentary pause in the hum of conversation as other teachers became intrigued. Caroline looked from me to Mark then blushed slightly.

"The last production of Hamlet I saw was very powerful because the ghost was portrayed as the imagining of a tortured mind, wracked with grief," she recovered herself. Others then began to contribute to the conversation and I was able to excuse myself and leave, nodding my gratitude to Chapman.

During the English lesson that afternoon, I was discussing poetry with the children and explaining that it was not necessary for verse to rhyme but that there ought to be a distinct rhythm. To my surprise, young Thomas Jenkins, who had been reasonably well-behaved and quiet for a change, suddenly raised his hand and asked what the purpose of poetry was. The question caught me off guard; I turned it around and asked the children what they thought. I was pleased with their answers about expressing emotion and creating a way of remembering special things and telling stories, illustrating an understanding perhaps beyond their years. It set me to thinking about what kind of poetry might be included in the book that April was determined we should search out.

As soon as the children had left for home I rang April on my mobile, telling her briefly what Chapman had said and suggesting we go to the local library to do some of our own research into the paranormal. She agreed to pick me up outside of school in five or ten minutes. As I left the building and headed towards the main gate Mark Chapman drove up alongside me, winding down his window to offer a ride home.

"I meant to catch you at lunch time to tell you that I have some friends who are really into the subject we were discussing at break, if you'd like to meet them sometime. And I'll look out those articles I was talking about before the end of the week."

"I'd appreciate that. Thanks for the offer of a lift too, but I'm already provided for tonight," I nodded at April's Volvo as she drew up.

Mark grinned. "Ah, now I see why you weren't interested in Caroline."

"Actually, I'm already married. April's a friend from college. She teaches at the grammar school down the road."

"Oh, I beg your pardon," he looked genuinely contrite. "Will Mrs. Kendall be with you when we all meet up at Canterbury on

Saturday?"

"It's unlikely. I'd rather not talk about it, if you don't mind." I knew it must seem as though I was snubbing him, but even after all this time I still couldn't bring myself to say that Kelly and I were separated.

"Sorry mate, I didn't mean to pry. I'd better go before I put my foot in it any further. See you tomorrow." He released his hand-break and, raising his hand in a gesture of farewell, drove off.

The library was a couple of miles from the school. It was built in the late nineteenth century by a particularly enlightened and wealthy local MP to house books for use by the 'general public', although one might surmise that not everybody would have been able to enjoy its facilities when it was first opened. It was very well stocked and included literature on most subjects, including the latest popular authors, as well as an amazing collection of valuable old books. It also boasted a superb computer suite, a relatively recent addition, which was just as well since I was forever having problems with my own machine at home. I kept promising to buy myself a slick new lap top but never got round to it somehow. Besides, Brian Cooke had been researching the possibility of providing staff with a school lap top each to help make more of their allotted PPA (planning, preparation and assessment) time. I was therefore in no hurry to shell out for my own personal newer technology just yet. April agreed to research using the internet, while I had a look at the library catalogue to see which books we might find most useful.

I sat before the computer monitor facing the door, the top half of which was glass so that I could see rows of books stretching to the end of the room beyond, merging into shadow. I tapped the keyboard in front of me and called up the library catalogue. Going to 'subject' I typed in various words, stopping each time to examine the books available under each. The lists appeared endless and I took a notebook from my brief case and noted down some of the titles and authors at random. After a while I glanced over at April, who appeared deeply engrossed in her task, and I heard the printer on the other side of the room whir into life as she requested print-outs of information. I turned back to my own computer, staring briefly out of the window at the top of the door as I did so. I frowned as a face passed by that I vaguely recognised but couldn't quite remember from where. I got up quietly, so as not to disturb April, and left the suite, wandering among the shelves of books beyond to see if I could surreptitiously study this person, but there appeared to be nobody else about. Between every two or three rows there were tables for people to sit and study if they wished but even these appeared deserted. Then I thought I caught the sound of low voices near the end of the long room and, feeling like a secret agent, I climbed the iron stairway to the second storey in the hope that I would be able to look down and see who was there.

I could just make out a group of people, a mixture of men and women of varying ages huddled together around one of the tables. One of the elder men turned and seemed to see me and although I couldn't clearly see his face, I was sure it was the person for whom I had been searching. He said something to the others and they promptly got up and left through another door at the end of the room. I was in two minds whether to follow but wasn't sure how to explain myself if I caught up with them, and anyway I felt I should get back to April.

"Have you found anything?" April emerged from the computer suite just as I was about to re-enter. She was carrying my briefcase and notebook.

"Not really. I saw a group of people I thought I knew but they've gone now, and it's annoying because I just can't seem to place where I've seen them before."

"I hate it when that happens. Look, I don't know how much of this will be useful. There was a lot of stuff about testing your own psychic abilities and web sites for further information but I just printed out a few recent essays and some extended definitions, that sort of thing. We need to pay at the front desk. Do you want to look for some books?"

"Not now. I think I'm done for tonight. I'm getting a bit hungry. Do you fancy fish and chips?"

Over our supper, which we ate sitting in April's car outside the chip shop, we discussed going to Canterbury to look for the poetry book. I was getting a bit disheartened; the whole thing now seemed little more than a silly fantasy created by an overactive imagination. In fact I'd been feeling a little that way for most of the day, if I were honest. April appeared as enthusiastic as ever though and I was glad of a friend I could really talk to, so I kept my thoughts to myself and agreed that she should pick me up early Saturday morning. She dropped me off at my house and handed over the bundle of photocopied sheets, for me to peruse at my leisure, before driving off.

I was unlocking my front door, struggling a little in the semi-darkness, when the wailing of what sounded like a young baby intruded on my thoughts. It seemed to be coming from the short privet hedge that separated my garden from that of the Scotts. I peered into the gloom but could see nothing and the noise stopped so, deciding it must be some nocturnal creature which had strayed into my garden and then out again, I continued to work with my keys and this time successfully opened my door. The howling suddenly recommenced and it really did seem unnervingly human. *Surely nobody would abandon a baby in my garden,* I thought, approaching the sound cautiously, fearful of treading on a child. The crying continued at a heartrending pitch and I could now just make out a small dark shape as I carefully parted the leaves.

Two luminous eyes suddenly stared devil-like at me and a black cat sprang, hissing and scratching, from beneath the hedge and shot into my house. I swore, sucking my hand where the animal had drawn blood, then hurried after the creature. The last thing I needed now was a cat setting off my allergy. I found him sitting under a kitchen chair, crouched low, watching for me and he immediately commenced the feline version of swearing at me in a low menacing whine. I tried to entice him back out of the house with various tutting sounds and other asinine noises but he became silent and simply regarded me for several minutes then, having decided I was more or less harmless, sat upright and proceeded to clean himself. Finally, I fetched two saucers and filled one with milk and the other with the tin of tuna I had planned to have in my sandwiches the next day. I pushed the saucers near his nose, trying to avoid contact while doing so. He ignored the milk but sniffed the tuna, so I slowly removed it and carried it, looking back at him as I went, to the doorstep. The temptation was too much and he slunk out of the kitchen after me. As soon as he began to eat, I went back inside the house and closed the door feeling victorious, despite the loss of tomorrow's lunch. I thought how Kelly would have laughed to see me.

I put the kettle on and sat slumped and dejected at the kitchen table, for all at once I felt as if I were in solitary confinement in some foreign prison cell, such were the waves of loneliness and isolation that swept over me. For a long time after Kelly left me I'd gone over the final conversations we'd shared, remembering how she empathised whenever I'd had a trying day at work, how she'd tell me all the details of a book she'd been reading or a film she'd seen, and I couldn't comprehend or accept that suddenly she didn't want to see me anymore or even talk to me. Gradually, I came to the conclusion she must never have loved me as I loved her, for she'd simply ignored me as if I no longer existed, while she apparently made a life somewhere else. I had dealt with this by pretending I hadn't thought of it; I kept busy, working long hours both at school and during my free time. I had taken up running, pushing myself harder and harder to go that extra few metres, that little bit faster, until the agony of an exhausted body seemed to numb the emotional despair to a point that it was almost cancelled out, at least while I ran. I stopped seeing many of the people we had spent time with socially and used my ambitions as a playwright to excuse myself. I gradually stopped haunting the places we had frequented and little by little stopped noticing the things in the house that spoke of her absence. I was surviving. It seemed the only thing I could not completely control was the occasional dream at night which would leave me aching with overwhelming grief the next day and a hopeless yearning for her to return.

I heard the cat crying once more outside my door and in this moment of weakness I let him back into the house. He appeared to understand and respect my desire to keep him from close contact, for he sat quite some way from my chair watching me, green eyes wary as if questioning my mood. I felt my face relax into a smile and he abruptly began to purr. He stood up, stretched and padded into the hallway, stopping to curl up by the door to the broom cupboard, where he immediately fell asleep. I didn't feel quite so alone anymore with him in the house and went up to bed myself, wondering where the cat had come from and whether his owners were missing him. I would have to put a card in the windows of nearby newsagents, if he stuck around, to see if anybody claimed him.

The next morning the cat sat patiently in the hall waiting for me to leave. As soon as I opened the door he trotted out, along the garden path and through a gap in the gate to pause on the pavement beyond. I slammed the door behind me and followed, reaching the gate just in time to hear two short, sharp barks and see the cat dash across the road. I flinched as a car narrowly missed him, and then I instinctively stamped on the end of a lead secured to the collar of a small dog about to scarper after the cat. It was just as well, for the dog would surely have been killed by the van that swept by in the wake of the car.

"Betsy!"

A short, slightly rounded woman, with a ruddy complexion and long, fine hair came running and panting towards me. She wore a long skirt and wax overcoat which valiantly withstood the muddy paws of the little sandy patched spaniel scooped into her arms from beside my feet. Another spaniel with dark markings watched the proceedings from the end of its own lead dangling from the woman's wrist. It grew impatient of the fuss being made of the other spaniel and finally barked. The woman put its companion down, patting both animals, and turned to me, a look of immense gratitude shining from her eyes.

"I don't know how I can ever thank you enough for saving Betsy from running into the road." She extended her hand, "By the way, I'm Abigail Maitland; I live in Albany Road."

"Peter Kendall. I'm afraid the cat your dog was chasing came from my house."

"Bitch." She chuckled at the shocked indignation that must have shown in my face for she quickly added, "Betsy and Trottwood are both females – bitches, not dogs."

"David Copperfield?"

"You're a Dickens fan too – how wonderful! I do love the classics, well most fiction actually. I work in the library so I guess you could say books are my livelihood. However, I love my two little girls here even more, so once again, thank you."

"No problem. Well, I'm sorry Mrs. er Abigail, I'm running a bit late. It's been nice talking to you though. Glad your dogs are okay."

"Bitches!" she called after me and I turned and waved an acknowledgment. The dark spaniel stared at me solemnly; for a moment I felt the hairs on the back of my neck rise, as some fleeting memory seeped into my mind like a wave, stealthily creeping towards the sandy shore, before retreating again. However, the sensation was soon forgotten as I succumbed to the day's events.

There was no sign of the cat when I got home from work that evening and I never saw him again. I did receive a card from Abigail Maitland though, thanking me yet again and inviting me to attend the book club that met once a month and would be gathering at her house at the end of the week. She wrote that she would understand if I didn't turn up but provided a telephone number in case I was interested.

After a light supper I had set to work reading through the material garnered by April at the library. My need to become completely familiar with all aspects of the primary school curriculum including Religious Education (particularly during teacher training), had inspired me to research numerous and sometimes seemingly curious aspects of various religions other than Christianity, and I had believed myself well informed in such matters. Nevertheless, by the time I was ready to retire to bed that night I was rather more knowledgeable than I had ever really been before. I had read about reincarnation and Karma, the significance of dreams to many faiths and their interpretation. I had also learned a little about astrology and fortune telling and read accounts of premonitions, which apparently saved people from being caught in disasters.

The following day Mark gave me a wad of papers about scientific research on some of the same subjects, so it was hardly surprising that I should begin to have strange dreams again. The only difference this time was that I was aware that some people would believe I was floating on the 'astral plane'. Further, they would probably consider the unseen, familiar companion to be my 'spirit guide'. I soon discovered, to my great satisfaction, that being aware of these things seemed to empower me, so that I was now able to manipulate what happened to me to some extent, and I could re-visit particular dreams and ask questions, although I rarely understood the answers.

I travelled back to the group on the hillside, digging for the cash box, and asked why the man's gift had been buried. I discovered that the box symbolised something else, as did its contents and the person for whom it was meant. I then understood the trainers, that I'd tried to re-bury, concerned my taking up running, when I was at my loneliest, and my attempts to repress the pain I was feeling with regard to Kelly. I wanted to know more about the cash box but was told to study the people in the group and then my alarm clock woke me before I had the opportunity to do so. I found a pen and paper and wrote notes in the form of a mind map.

On Friday evening I decided to cancel the appointment with Phillip Wells until after I had been to Canterbury with April to discover whether the book really did exist. I called into the therapist's office in person to apologise. He looked at me steadily, as I made my excuses, and then told me that he had read my dream diary and felt it rather urgent that we should discuss the contents. From the moment of my arrival I'd felt ill at ease, as if he was summing me up or analysing me. Of course, that was part of his job, but I didn't particularly want him to be doing it right at that moment, when I wasn't on his couch. I insisted I hadn't time to attend a session with him until Monday evening and he finally agreed and told me to see myself out as he had a telephone call to make. As I crossed the, for once deserted, reception area to the door leading out onto the street, I realised his office door hadn't latched properly and remained slightly ajar, so I went back to pull it shut. It was then that I overheard Wells asking to speak to the police and mentioning my name. I stood still for several seconds, listening.

"Yes. I've been seeing Peter Kendall on and off for several years in connection with severe emotional stress. Well, he told me he was having problems coping because his wife had left him. However, I now have reason to believe that he might have murdered her."

Chapter Nine

"April, where are you?"

"I've been having a drink with a colleague. I'm on my way home now. What's up?"

"I'm waiting outside your house. Hurry up, it's bloody freezing. I'll explain when you get here."

I snapped my mobile phone shut and stuffed my hands into my mackintosh pockets. It had started to drizzle and water trickled inside the collar and down my neck. I hunched my shoulders and shuffled from one foot to the other. A police patrol car appeared at the end of the road and drove slowly towards me. I slid round the corner to the side of the house and out of sight. The car passed by without stopping and my accelerated heartbeat slowed to a more normal rhythm as I exhaled, emptying my lungs of the breath I'd been holding. April's Volvo drew up and I waved and waited at the front door for her to join me. She looked curious and a little perturbed but waited until we were settled with hot drinks before asking questions. I explained about my visit to Phillip Wells and how I'd overheard his conversation with the police on the telephone.

"Why does he suddenly think you murdered Kelly?"

"It must be the dream diary. I guess some of those dreams do sound a bit suspect, digging up her trainer and trying to cover it up again, tombs, and then finally seeing her and a mere touch of my hand makes her scream and disintegrate into thousands of tiny pieces."

"Ughh, is that the sort of thing you've been dreaming?" April shuddered and I pressed my lips together in annoyance.

"April, I told you that last bit the other night and you just thought it was telepathy then."

"Sorry Peter, but I think you're right. Your dreams do sound a little suspicious."

"I'm hoping the police will know how to locate Kelly and talk to her again but in the meantime I'd rather not take any chances. Can I bunk here for the night? I need to see if we can get that book. If we do find it then there's a chance I will see Kelly at the church at Stillbury on Sunday. If not I'll go home and wait to see what happens."

"I think you should go to the meeting place even if we don't find the book. You've nothing to lose. I'll fetch some bedding and you can kip on the sofa tonight; I'd let you have the spare room but it's full of paperwork and books. I don't suppose the police are really looking for you just yet, I think they only work that fast on TV cop shows, but we may as well err on the side of caution. Besides, I'd like your advice on something."

She went off to fetch pillows and a duvet while I finished my drink and took off my shoes, stretching out on the sofa with my hands behind my head as I stared up at the ceiling. April was soon back, dumping her burden on an arm chair and sliding down to sit on the floor near me, beside the couch.

"Pete, how do you cope without sex?"

"What?" I sat up startled and not a little alarmed.

"Don't worry. I'm not bisexual and I don't think I'd fancy you even if I was. I'm just curious."

I wasn't absolutely convinced and my reply was therefore

86

wary. "I'm not sure I want to talk about this, April, it's making me uncomfortable." I rested on one elbow. She waited. "Well, I throw myself into my work, I go running and occasionally I lose myself listening to classical music. I'm not going to go into it any further than that. If you want to imagine me with one night stands or prostitutes, that's fine by me. Why do you want to know anyway?"

"The girl I'm seeing."

"The ice skater?"

"Yup, she's gone off to stay with her parents for a while. Says she wants to take things slowly. I really like her a lot but you know me, I'm not the patient type."

"Now there's a story for a playwright…"

"Don't you dare," she jumped up and grabbed the bedding, flinging it at me, laughing. One of the pillows hit my head and I threw it back, trying to untangle the duvet in the process. She caught the pillow and hugged it to herself for a moment before calmly handing it back.

"It's just as well she's gone off on holiday to see her parents if I'm going to be spending the weekend helping you out."

"You are much more patient and understanding than you give yourself credit for, you know. Think of the way you've listened to me, especially this past week or so."

She smiled and proceeded to tuck the duvet about my shoulders, and then kissed my forehead in a matter of fact manner before switching off the lamp light.

"See you in the morning."

"Hey, can't a bloke get something to eat around here?"

"There's some left over casserole in the oven you can warm up if you like. I'm all in and I need my beauty sleep. Goodnight."

I considered getting up but was cosy by then and couldn't be bothered, so I turned on my side and was soon fast asleep. It seemed but a few moments before I was dragged out of the depths of oblivion by an insistent prodding at my shoulder.

"Wake up lazy bones." April nudged me with her knee; she had two steaming mugs of tea in her hands. I rubbed my eyes, squinting at her. "Hurry up – it's gone 8 o'clock. Pity you didn't fancy the casserole; there's only muesli or toast for Breakfast and you won't have time for that if you don't get a move on."

I sat up and took one of the mugs from her. "Ouch, that's hot!"

"Peter, you slept in your clothes!" she cried, exasperated. "You'd better let me have that shirt and I'll try and freshen it up while you shower. Honestly, you're hopeless. Shame you didn't bring some clean kit with you." I pulled my shirt off over my head, grumbling all the while about her bossiness, while she held my tea. She cautiously sniffed the proffered shirt. "Shouldn't be too bad," she decided. "Hurry up!"

Forty minutes later, we were heading along the A2 towards Canterbury. There wasn't too much traffic about at that time in the morning so we made good time and were soon pulling into one of the few roads available for parking that wasn't reserved for residents, and yet was within walking distance of the city centre.

We left the car and cut across Westgate Gardens, enjoying the sparkling morning sunlight reflected on the river and the fresh smell of trees and newly cut grass. There were a number of pedestrians and shoppers milling about, but the streets were far from crowded yet. Gulls cried, whirling above the street, giving the false impression that the city was a seaport and somehow injecting a holiday atmosphere into the visit.

April and I peered at shop fronts, looking for signs of books, and we meandered down side roads. Eventually we came across a recently opened second-hand store which had originally been some sort of craft or mystical shop. This was evident from the weathered headboard above the display window which had yet to be repainted. It proclaimed in fancy gold writing: *Mystic Clara's trinkets –tarot readings available by appointment.*

"What do you think?" April asked.

"I think this might be the place." I pointed at the sign which had one or two stars and a crescent moon dotted around the words by way of decoration and underneath several small lines, protruding from a larger horizontal line. "That's identical to the graffiti that was daubed on my lounge wall with green paint – it's too much of a coincidence."

"Too bad the place is closed."

April cupped her hands round her eyes and pressed her face up against the window, trying to peer inside. I followed suit. The walls were lined with shelving filled with books of every shape and size and there were several boxes overflowing with paperbacks on the floor. An open door revealed an uncarpeted stairway sharply lit up by a fluorescent tube light but the place looked deserted. I ignored the closed sign and tried the door, shaking the handle roughly when it refused to yield. There was no notice of opening times. I kicked the bottom of the door in frustration.

"Hey, you'll get us arrested. Come on let's go and find some tea. Perhaps it will be open later." April pulled at my arm and reluctantly I allowed her to lead me away.

I didn't want to risk returning to my own house before I'd had a chance to meet up with Kelly on Sunday, just in case the police were about, so I knew I needed to buy a fresh set of clothes – especially if I was to attend the teacher's send off that evening. My credit card was about to take a whacking and I needed to draw out some ready cash from the bank too. We returned a couple of hours later, carrying bags from Burtons and one or two other retailers to find the book shop still shut. However, there was now a sheet of paper taped to the inside of the door which stated that the business was closed temporarily due to staff illness but that the shop would be open again on Monday. I hammered on the door with my fists.

"There must be someone in there because the light's still on."

"You're right. I think I can see somebody moving about. Hang on they're coming to the door."

"I'm sorry, we're closed. Please go away." The fifty-something, balding man looked me up and down coldly and was about to shut the door on us again when April pushed her way in front of me.

"I do apologise for my husband's impatience. We were wondering whether you purchase books from private collectors or take donations."

"I'm not buying today." The man made to close the door again but April was persistent, inserting her body into the gap.

"Please, we aren't trying to sell. My aunt sold some books to an unspecified shop in Canterbury and accidentally included a poetry book which was of great sentimental value to her. It belonged to her daughter, killed in an accident. We just wanted to see if you had it and if so whether we might buy it back. We've been trolling around bookshops all morning. Please, might we just take a quick look? My aunt's inconsolable." She smiled sweetly at the chap and nudged me.

"Yes. We wouldn't be long and we'd be so grateful. We're both teachers," I added hopefully as an afterthought. The shopkeeper shrugged and stepped to one side to allow us access, telling us that the most recently acquired books were on the second storey. He re-latched the door behind us then went to the back of the shop and began sorting through one of the boxes. I followed April up the stairs.

"What's being teachers got to do with anything?" she hissed at me as soon as we were out of earshot.

"I'm sorry; I thought it might sound respectable, as if we'd be good future customers who'd recommend other prospective bookbuyers to the shop. Besides, I can't tell bare-faced lies as easily as you can. Since when have we been married? And where does this aunt mourning the deceased cousin live?"

She poked her tongue out at me, and then turned to survey the room we'd entered. "Where do we start?"

"We need to find the sections on world religions and history. I know," I sighed as April raised her eyebrows. "But that is where Kelly told me to look for it." I bent my head to one side as I walked along the rows of books, scanning book spines. April called out that she'd found the right area and I joined her to check the titles. There were books on Judaism, Christianity, Hinduism, Sikhism, even books on the occult and witchcraft, but we could find no poetry book.

The floorboards creaked behind us and the shopkeeper enquired whether we had managed to find what we were looking for, adding that he really needed to close the shop up now as he had other business to attend to. I ran my fingertips lightly over the top shelf one last time. It was then that I felt a small, slim book wedged between two large volumes entitled *World Religions and their origins.* I pulled one of the volumes out slightly and prised the small book from its hiding place. It was little more than a hard-backed exercise book, the cover dark blue and sprinkled with stars. I turned it over in my hands and realised I'd been holding it upside down for on the other side a large star decorated the centre of the cover. My breath caught in my throat. I held the book up for the shopkeeper to see, shaking it affectionately in my hand. He took it from me, flipping it open to inspect the contents; to my surprise it appeared to be handwritten rather than printed. With the most cursory appraisal he snapped it shut and handed it back.

"Let's call it twenty-five quid," he said.

"Twenty-five pounds? That's outrageous!" April protested.

I quickly took out my wallet and paid over the notes without comment. April was furious with me and made certain I was aware of the fact once we were back out on the street, the book safely tucked inside my coat pocket. I knew it would have been a waste of time arguing with the fellow, though. He'd realised we wanted the book and if we argued too much he might have raised the price or become suspicious, thinking it could be valuable. Then he might easily have refused to sell. I explained to April that I couldn't afford to take the risk of losing the purchase and we walked the rest of the way to her Volvo in silence, April still sulking. However, her curiosity got the better of her by the time we were seated in the car and she insisted on taking a look at the book. She skimmed over the writing, turning the pages quickly and handed it back to me grimacing.

"I rather think he got the better part of the bargain," she sniffed, glaring at me before starting the car engine. I replaced the book in my coat pocket, already having decided I would study it when I was able to sit quietly and give it my full attention.

April had agreed with me that I should stay at her place until Sunday evening and she had given me a spare key. However unlikely a murder suspect I liked to believe myself to be, the police may wish to question me if they hadn't been successful in establishing Kelly's whereabouts, and I wasn't sure I could give them any suitable answers at present. Now, as April drove, I called my house answering service, and listened for any messages on my mobile. There were two, one from Phillip Wells confirming my appointment for Monday (*at least he was still expecting me to be at liberty,* I thought with some satisfaction) and one from Caroline Lyman, reminding me that the staff would be meeting at the Irish pub near Westgate in Canterbury at 7:00 p.m. I glanced sideways at April's sullen face and decided it would take some charm to persuade her to lend me the Volvo for the evening, while she was in her present mood, and I wasn't sure I had the patience. I decided perhaps it would be better to catch the train, that way I would have an excuse to leave at a reasonable time and not have to worry about my alcohol intake.

I offered to pay April for her choice of takeaway food by way of a peace offering but she muttered something about needing to eat more healthily. When we arrived back at her home, she made a cheese and chicken salad and placed the fruit bowl in the centre of the table as an indication of dessert. We didn't talk much during the meal and after the plates were cleared and washed, she sat down with a couple of magazines and switched the television on, a sure sign that she wished to be left alone. I excused myself and went to wash and shave and get ready to go out. However, as I was about to leave to catch the train she called out to me to have a good time, so I went back into her lounge and handed her the little book.

"Put that somewhere safe for me and we'll have a natter when I get back. Promise I won't be late." She looked up and smiled and I kissed her on the cheek and left to travel to the cathedral city for the second time that day.

***

"The train at platform 1 will call at Faversham, Selling, Canterbury-East and Dover Priory…"

I sprinted, lunging forward and hitting the button to prevent the electronic doors closing just as the guard blew his whistle. I managed to haul myself aboard the train, escaping with only a slightly bruised thigh caught in the sliding doors due to the guard engaging the over-ride mechanism in an attempt to foil my efforts. The guard shouted at me furiously, but I ignored him and walked along the crowded carriage, taking off my coat as I went in an attempt to cool down while looking for an empty seat. I found two and took the one nearest the window, throwing my overcoat into the luggage rack above my head as I did so. The seat next to me was very soon taken by a young woman with a toddler, who pulled her folded pushchair and shopping bags near to her feet so they would not completely obstruct the walkway. I looked up at the screen of the message board at the end of the carriage, constantly displaying a stream of station names at which the train would be stopping. It was then I spotted a figure I recognised at once, opening the door leading to the next carriage.

My lanky spy 'friend', wearing a long, smart, grey overcoat and hat was right before my eyes. I was now certain he was the man I had seen emerging from my house the day I had come home to find it redecorated. I tried to jump up, lost my balance, bumped my head on the window and knocked the woman next to me in the face with my elbow. I apologised in panic and, amid much grumbling and protest, scrambled past her and the little girl to pursue my prey.

Unfortunately, I had been delayed too long and though I examined the faces of as many passengers as possible in the next two carriages, I could not find him. The train was nearing my station, so reluctantly I returned to my seat to fetch my coat. The woman was organising her child and possessions and was not amused that I wanted to reach over her head. My coat was gone. I didn't expect her to offer any assistance but I enquired of her anyway if she'd seen anyone take it. She shook her head and trudged off down the walkway loaded down with possessions, the child trailing behind. I could feel somebody's eyes on me and I looked across to the seat on the other side of the train to find a young man with long, shaggy hair and beard to match, watching me with interest.

"If you're looking for your coat mate, tall, skinny bloke took it."

"When was that? Did you see where he went?"

"He reached up from behind that woman while she was organising her kid so I guess she didn't see. Anyway, he got off the train a second ago."

I thanked him and was only just in time to descend from the train before it pulled out of the station. I looked up and down the platform but there was no sign of the thief. There was nothing I could do but report my loss to the stationmaster and that would make me late so I decided against it. At least I had my wallet with me. I left the station and crossed the road, taking the bridge to the path along the city wall, looking about me all the time in the hope I might catch a glimpse of the lofty man, but he had vanished. I was feeling really annoyed with myself and puzzled as to how he'd managed to get past me while I'd been searching for him on the train. I wondered whether he'd been following me all along and if he could see me now as I walked. I wasn't succumbing to paranoia, in fact I decided I found it slightly amusing, in an ironic sort of way, that he'd managed to purloin my favourite, shabby raincoat, when his own was really so much more prepossessing. I was fairly confident that he would be disappointed with his prize once he'd searched the pockets.

Despite my little adventure on the train, the evening went very well and everyone seemed to be in fine spirit, joking and telling stories about the teacher who was moving on to another school. She was presented with a photograph album, card and flowers and she made an appropriate little speech of thanks. The food was good and the wine flowed. Just before 10:00 p.m. somebody proposed going on to a nightclub. Mark pointed out that it was raining hard outside as people were pouring into the bar wet and dishevelled. I had thought it a good time to make my farewells but hesitated, having no coat. Caroline leaned forward and grasped the coat hanging over the back of her seat, handing it to me. To my utter amazement it was the one that had been stolen on the train. I checked the pockets and found the receipt for the book I'd purchased earlier in the day.

"How did my coat get there?"

"Well, I assume you put it there earlier."

I decided against trying to explain my bewilderment. I scanned the bar then hastily donned my coat and wished everyone a good night. As I pushed my way through the doors out onto the dimly lit street, now shining with the recent rainfall, I was no longer amused. Instead I felt jumpy, vulnerable and stone cold sober. Few people were about because of the inclement weather so I hurried through the city centre, taking the footpaths through the subways, where thankfully buskers still performed, and along the main road rather than the city wall. I needn't have been so cautious; my walk was uneventful and I was in plenty of time for the train. I reached April's house just after 11:00 p.m. and was surprised to see her car missing. I let myself into the house and found a note for me pinned to the refrigerator:

My Ice Maiden called and invited me to her parents' for the rest of the weekend, so if you want my bed tonight you're welcome. There's plenty of hot water and food in the fridge if you're still hungry. The book's in the kitchen drawer. Will try to get back to take you to Stillbury on Sunday evening but in case I'm not able to, there's a bus timetable pinned up in my spare room. Ring me

95

Monday if I don't see you before.

April

I pulled open the nearest kitchen drawer and shuffled through the contents. No book. I opened the next and the next until I had searched them all to no avail. I rang April's mobile but was put straight onto voicemail; she had switched her telephone off. All I could do was hope that she would either call me or arrive back in time to accompany me to Stillbury. I thought of the 'spy' and the episode with my coat and shivered. On impulse I hurried around the house, switching on all the lights, checking the windows and locking all the doors, for I was convinced that the stranger had been looking for the book and I didn't want him to invade April's home. As I eventually made my way up to bed, I hoped fervently that he hadn't already been to the house, seen the note and found the book.

Chapter Ten

On Sunday morning I braved the spare bedroom which April had converted to a study, in search of the bus timetable. It was indeed pinned to the wall on the bottom of a cork-faced notice board, which was a collage of postcards, photographs and notes. However, the timetable was unfortunately a year out of date. I waited until lunchtime for April to return home and, when she didn't appear, decided I would have to go back to my own house where I knew I had recent copies of both bus and train schedules. I was less worried about the police turning up now; if they'd really wanted to find me I was sure they would have done so. Besides, I had made several unsuccessful attempts at contacting April on her mobile and was becoming quite agitated because I didn't have the book, so the last thing I wanted to worry about was not being able to get to the appointed place by 5:00 p.m.

It took about forty minutes to stroll back home and I let myself into the house without incident. I was trying to recall just where I'd left those timetables and was halfway up the stairs, when the doorbell rang. I froze for a moment and then, feeling slightly nauseas with apprehension, I went down and opened the door. I was relieved to see Jem standing on the doorstep, rather than some burly officers, and my expression must have revealed my relief. However, this didn't seem to surprise Jem.

"I bet you were worried about your car," my neighbour beamed, dangling a set of keys in front of my nose. "But it's okay; I talked the lad into letting me sign for it. He was only a kid. I felt quite sorry for him when he realised you weren't in. You should have seen the panic on his face."

"Jem, what are you talking about?"

"Your new Metro," he waved his hand in the general direction of a small, red car.

"But I was going to get a Toyota…"

"That's not what it says on the paperwork." Jem pulled some folded sheets from his pocket and handed them over. "I must say, Pete, you're getting a bit forgetful these days. Fancy forgetting your car was being delivered yesterday."

I was about to protest that I hadn't ordered a new car yet, when my eye caught sight of the scrawl at the bottom of the page I'd been studying incredulously. It was undoubtedly my signature. I refolded the papers and grinned at Jem, shaking the keys, as if delighted. "Just kidding, Mate. Thanks for taking delivery. I kind of got held up at a friend's house."

"Woman, was it?"

"You know how it is. Anyway, thanks again. I owe you a drink."

Satisfied, he went back next door and I stood for some minutes inspecting the neat little Metro parked at the side of the road, in the same position that my old mini had previously stood. It wasn't the smart and spacious, midnight blue Toyota I'd envisaged driving in future and I was baffled as to how the showroom had managed to get my signature but it was a nice car and since it was there I might as well use it to get to Stillbury.

To reach the little Norman church of St. Lawrence I drove along the A-road in the direction of Mentorham, taking the sign-posted turn-off which crossed the opposite half of a busy dual carriageway, to ascend a winding lane set on an incline. I turned right at the junction near the top, slowly motoring towards the ancient Norman building that dominated the landscape. I parked the car on a grass verge close to the church gate. I was early but it was worth the wait just to have a while to indulge myself viewing the breathtaking landscape across the Swale.

I'd walked slowly round the church twice before I remembered an old wives' tale that if you circumnavigated a church three times anti-clockwise you could call up the devil, so I came to an abrupt halt near the church door feeling rather foolish for being superstitious. There was a heavenly smell of green foliage and damp earth and I began to enjoy the oddest tingling sensation through the whole of my body. I moved nearer the door and it stopped. I went back to my original position and it recurred but I had to stand in exactly the right place, overlooking a dip in the ground beyond a crumbling wall, separating the church land from an old orchard. I wasn't sure whether such things as ley lines really existed, but I knew some people believed in natural energies emanating from deep beneath the planet's surface. I wondered briefly if these people had experienced something akin to this feeling. Wasn't it true that churches had often been built on sites already sacred for some reason or another? I told myself I was imagining things and went to the gate to look up and down the road for any sign of Kelly. I could see nobody and therefore flinched in astonishment when someone tapped me on the shoulder.

With a sharp expletive I fought to recover myself, then "Frank Rowell. I haven't seen you in a while!"

"Hello Peter, it's good to see you. Did you bring the book?"

I stared at him suspiciously. "Where's Kelly?"

"It's rather complicated and I haven't much time to explain," he looked carefully left and right, searching the deserted lane. "I'm afraid Kelly couldn't make it but we have to have the book. It's urgent. Have you got it?"

"No. Not with me. And even if I did have it, I'm not sure I would give it to you. I want to see Kelly."

"I'm sorry old boy but without the book that just will not be possible."

"What's that supposed to mean?" I raised myself to my full height and stared very hard at him with the gaze I usually reserved for badly behaved pupils. He stared back for long seconds then appeared to come to a decision.

"If I can prove to you that I'm here on Kelly's behalf, would you hand over the book then? I mean, if you knew she was in trouble and the book could help her?"

"I expect so. I don't know. For crying out loud, Frank, what's going on? When she went missing you and Pauline swore you knew nothing about it. Why couldn't Kelly come?"

"Peter, you'll just have to trust me. Meet me back here tomorrow evening at the same time, with the book. I promise I'll do my best to satisfy your curiosity then." He turned on his heel and began to walk briskly away.

"Now wait a minute …" I started to follow him. My mobile phone rang and I stopped briefly to remove it from my pocket and take the call. It was April. I continued to stride in the direction Frank Rowell had taken while listening to April. She merely wanted to let me know she was now home and I hastily re-pocketed the telephone, quickening my step further. I hurried round a bend in the lane, expecting to see Frank ahead but he was gone. I cursed, realising he must have had a car parked nearby which I'd been too distracted to hear. There was nothing I could do except return to April's house.

She was waiting impatiently at the lounge window when I got back. "Smashing little car – thought you were going for a Toyota this time?"

"Apparently not. April, what did you do with the book?" She frowned and went into the kitchen. I followed and watched as she opened a kitchen drawer.

"Here it is, just where I told you. Oh, hang on a minute. The telephone rang as I was about to put it in here. Now, what did I do with it?" She pressed her palm against her forehead then pushed her fringe from out of her eyes. "I know." She tripped back into the lounge to the cabinet on which the telephone stood and opened it, taking out the blue, star spangled book. "Ta raa! Oh, Peter I am sorry," her face fell as realisation dawned. "Was Kelly mad that you didn't have it with you?"

I took the book and sighed. "Is there any tea in the pot? I'll tell you all about it but I need something to perk me up a bit."

I flopped down on the sofa and began relating the events of the day, calling through to the kitchen as she clattered about. I was in the process of telling her about the mysterious way in which the car had apparently been purchased in my name, when she re-appeared and placed a tray laden with tea things on the coffee table. There was a plate of biscuits and a Victoria sponge, cut into triangles, and she had decided to use her best bone-china tea cups; it was all very civilized. She handed me my tea and a plate, and took a slice of the cake for herself, interrupting my intended compliments.

"What was the date on the order form?" She carefully sat in a chair facing me, one foot tucked up underneath her.

"Yesterday, I'm pretty sure it was dated for yesterday and there was a time on the form. I think it was 10:00 a.m. I'll have a look later to check."

"Well you certainly couldn't have signed it – you were in Canterbury with me, or heading that way. We could go back to the garage tomorrow evening and sort it out. There's no reason why you can't still have your Toyota."

That's the other thing. Tomorrow evening I have to go back to Stillbury. Kelly didn't show up today, but an old chap, I once met with her years ago, claimed to have come for the book on her behalf. I have to see him again to try and find out where she is and what's going on."

"I think you should take that book into school tomorrow and get it photocopied," April observed, biting into her cake once more and chewing thoughtfully.

"That's a good idea. I'm looking forward to having a read of it later. Now, that's enough of my problems. Tell me all about your trip."

I had decided to stay at April's house for one more night and as I lay alone on the sofa later, I opened the book and began to decipher the inky scrawl which filled the pages with verse. I didn't recognise any of the poems and after a brief preliminary scan of the text I went back to the beginning and read with more focus.

The verses did not appear to be written in any particular poetic style but seemed to be simple, some with common rhyming patterns, others free verse, each quite distinctive. The first poem described a meeting, or rather the sighting of a woman who had fascinated and inspired the writer, filling him with a sense of yearning and wonder. It was a little clumsy and rather old fashioned in style and was followed by an account of friendship blossoming and eventually the realisation of love. The third was a romantic sonnet, serenading a woman's beauty and perfection but then the fourth spoke of unrequited passion and the pain of rejection. The next didn't mention the human muse and, although the short poem seemed inspired by self-pity, I could almost sense the loneliness and desperation of the poet persona. This seemed to mark a turning point and the poetry after that gradually degenerated into a dark and sinister spewing of resentment and obsession and I could no longer empathise with the writer or the person whose feelings he described. Tiredly, I closed the book and tucked it under my pillow and then turned onto my side and fell into a deep and dreamless sleep.

I wait for you. I long for you. How can you not now come?
Oh write to me, admit you care. Leave me not so alone.
I weep for you, cannot sleep, for you, cannot eat, will surely die.
You haunt my every waking thought. Please do not mean 'goodbye'.

Try again. I know we can reach him…

Please be careful…

"Peter. Oh, for Heaven's sake, what's happened to you?"

I squinted as the lounge filled with light. Bleary-eyed I focussed on April standing across the room from the sofa staring, her eyes dark and frightened.

Chapter Eleven

"What is it, woman?" Grumpily, I tried to raise myself but felt a blinding pain in my forehead. My hand flew to my face in response but then, puzzled, I held it in front of my eyes – it was sticky and wet, smeared with blood. April recovered from her initial shock and sped into action, finding a clean tea towel in the kitchen which she hastily wrung under the cold water tap; within seconds she was wiping my face with the cool cloth.

"Nosebleed", she explained, authoritatively as she went about cleaning me up. "It's stopped now. Funny, I came down for a glass of milk and I could have sworn I saw…well, it doesn't matter."

"What did you think you saw?" I took the cloth from her and pressed it against my forehead. "Have you any paracetamol? My head's killing me."

"Well, I know it sounds daft but I thought there were fireflies or sparks or something hovering above you." She fetched some tablets from the kitchen. "It was probably my eyes adjusting to the hall light while I was still half-asleep."

"I think I might have been having one of those nightmares but I can't seem to remember…"

"Have you had your blood pressure checked recently? You know, that could cause all sorts of problems."

"I'm fine, April, really. I just need to go back to sleep." I handed the tea towel back to her. "Thanks for the cloth and painkillers. Sleep well."

I lay back down, my back purposely to her and she took the hint. Perhaps she was right about the blood pressure, yet there was that odd metallic taste in my mouth again and the urge to listen to music was so great I clenched the duvet to my mouth and bit on it.

A horrible idea began to form in my head. Supposing it wasn't blood pressure at all but something more sinister? What if I had a brain tumour or something? It would certainly account for some of the strange events that had occurred recently. However, the hard angular edges of the poetry book, stashed beneath my pillow, provided some reassurance. I recalled the events leading to its discovery in the bookshop, which had involved April to some extent. I wasn't completely alone. I decided I must look into getting some serious medical check-ups *after* I'd met with Frank again and discovered just exactly what he knew about Kelly and why a tatty and faded, handwritten poetry book was so important. With this resolution in mind I closed my eyes, relaxed my muscles and was soon fast asleep.

***

"Oh, poetry! That should be fun. Whose work is this then? It's surely not from one of your lot?"

"Actually my class are quite astute where poetry's concerned!" I carefully took the sheet away from Caroline and gathered the sheaf of paper from the photocopier, whisking the book from beneath the protective shield as I did so.
"How's the romance going then?"

She stiffened, her body language revealing her annoyance. "I haven't time to gossip. Some of us have got work to do." She pushed past me and began leafing through a book of science activity sheets with grave concentration. I grinned to myself – all was obviously not well in paradise – and made my way back to my classroom, almost colliding with Mark in the corridor.

"I've just seen your paramour! She's in a bit of a prickly mood."

"That isn't funny." He continued walking but then stopped, turning back to stare hard at me. "You knew she was married. Why the hell didn't you tell me?"

"Separated, Mate. I don't think it's the same thing," I raised my hands in a mock gesture of innocent protest, almost dropping some of the sheets I'd been photocopying.

"Oh really! That's not the impression I got when I mentioned *your* ex." He strode off, leaving me feeling slightly ashamed.

***

I waited at the Church gate. The early evening was cool and grey, the sky a melancholy skating rink in which seagulls glided and turned, crying their songs of anguish above the fields across the way. I felt restless and resigned all at once – exactly as I'd felt for so long after Kelly first disappeared from our home. Part of me was simmering with a quiet, tense anger that she should put me through this. The other part remembered her kindness, sweet generosity and loving spirit and waited impatiently for her to come back to me, explain, hold me again, warming my soul with her words of love and melting the aching misery inside. I was so lonely.

People say they get over grief (and it *is* grief when someone abandons you) by keeping themselves busy, and I suppose it's true to some extent although for me work became difficult for a while; I couldn't concentrate and found it hard to focus when I needed to. I even remember dully thinking that I would lose my job if I didn't pull myself together. At least when someone dies there is no chance of reconciliation, no suddenly happening upon the beloved by accident in a shopping mall, no insistent glimmer of hope that refuses to die, whispering that one day they will reappear. The bereaved may suffer the odd shock of thinking they see the object of their affection in the street only to find it is somebody else. They may occasionally set an extra place at the meal table, half-expecting the loved one still to come through the back door at any moment and drop a bag on the floor and keys on the kitchen table, until they remember their loss. Yet ultimately, deep down, they know the one person they long to see never will arrive home. And in that sorrow, that heartrending grief, there is a kind of peace.

I sighed, mentally saluting all the people like me who have been left waiting. I tried to imagine what it would be like to walk away from one's life with all of its tedious day to day concerns and the people that share them and just vanish, start life afresh somewhere else. How strong or weak must you need to be to send no comforting reassurance to those left behind that you hadn't been taken against your will, murdered, or that you hadn't met with some sort of accident? How selfish? A policeman once told me that he felt like a killer whenever he went to deliver news of a fatality because before he arrived, in the minds of the people to whom he spoke, the deceased was still alive, walking around, laughing, talking, eating; he felt it was his words that really deprived them of their loved one. Perhaps there is some truth in the sentiment that ignorance is bliss, but I could still empathise with those who just wanted to know what had happened, even if that meant the certainty of the end of a life.

I wait for you. I long for you. How can you not now come?
Oh write to me, admit you care. Leave me not so alone.
I weep for you, cannot sleep, for you, cannot eat, will surely die.
You haunt my every waking thought. Please do not mean 'goodbye'.

The words drifted into my consciousness, as I stood there, pondering and wondering whether this meeting was going to be just another dead end, another hope doused with disappointment.

My thoughts were interrupted by the sound of approaching footsteps and I turned as Frank lifted an arm in greeting. Deep in my overcoat pocket my fingers felt for the pocked surface of the poetry book. I moved away from the church gate and stood, feet slightly apart, body rigid, prepared for confrontation. I was therefore mildly surprised when Frank called out in a friendly manner, jogging the last few steps towards me.

"If we follow the lane down further there's a small entrance to the ground at the back of the church."

"Why are we going there?"

He slowed to a walk. "You'll see. You do have the book, don't you?"

"We'll talk about the book when I know what's going on?"

Frank said nothing further but strode purposely on ahead. I followed, slightly baffled and more than a little intrigued. After a while we reached the opening he had spoken of but it was narrow and overgrown with brambles and nettles. We pushed our way through, sinking into tangled orchard grass, wading past barren and despairing trees, their low branches struggling to retain freedom from the raggedly rising floor of weeds and couch. After a while the ground cover flattened out, trodden down by other feet that must have passed that way. Frank's pace slackened slightly. All I could see ahead in the growing gloom of dusk was similar terrain – a huge jungle of neglected orchard. At that moment I became aware of the hum of an engine and a black, shiny monster of a four wheel drive bumped its way across the ground towards us. Before it got close enough for me to see who was inside, Frank stopped and drew a scarf from his coat pocket.

"Peter, I'm afraid I'm going to have to blindfold you for the next part."

"Not bloody likely!" I exclaimed, taking a step back. Frank merely held the scarf out to me.

"If you want to see Kelly you have no choice. Everything will be explained in due course. Have some faith, old boy. Please. It will only be for a very short while."

It seemed a waste of time to argue for he seemed adamant. I removed my glasses, wiped the lenses and put them carefully into my breast pocket. "You aren't tying me." I wanted to make sure. "And you aren't having my mobile telephone, either."

Frank snorted. "Really Peter! Do you honestly believe we are trying to kidnap you? What would be the point of that?"

I didn't like his calm retort, as if *I* was the one being unreasonable. "Well, this is hardly normal, is it?"

I snatched the scarf and crossly proceeded to wind it about my head. Frank checked it was in place properly, over my eyes, and tightened the knot then took my arm to guide me towards the vehicle. As I slid across the seat and heard the clunk of the door close, the scent of Lily of the Valley wafted towards me and I thought that the silent driver must be female. I heard another door being opened and felt the seat sag slightly, and the upholstery creak, as Frank climbed into the back beside me, asking if I was okay. I was interested to hear a low male voice make some inaudible remark before the vehicle began to manoeuvre again, revealing that there must be at least two other people in the vehicle with us.

We travelled, tumbling and lurching uncomfortably along for a very short while, and then with a final growl of the engine the vehicle lurched sideways, throwing me hard against the door; it righted itself and was then gliding along a smooth surface and I assumed we were on a road. It's difficult to say how long we were travelling; it could have been an hour or forty minutes. Nobody spoke and I heard no other traffic on the road, just the steady purr of the four wheel drive. My face began to itch and my eyes water beneath the prickly fabric of the scarf. It was a ridiculous precaution: I was practically blind without my glasses anyway so I wouldn't have been able to see where we were going. As if he'd read my thoughts, Frank suddenly reached over and pulled the scarf from my face. To my surprise we were in total darkness.

"What are you doing? Are you crazy? If we don't use headlights we'll crash!"

I didn't have time to panic further, as the vehicle slowed to a stop and Frank and the others proceeded to get out. I tried my own door and it was unlocked so I followed suit. It was a cloudy evening; there were now no stars, no moon, in fact no discernible light anywhere that I could make out. The woman struck a match. It went out. She lit another. This time a light appeared a short distance in front of us and it was towards this we began to walk.

Chapter Twelve

We trudged silently along, a shadowy group, disturbed only by the natural small noises of the night and as we neared the light I realised it was somebody standing very still waiting with a large, battery-powered torch. Closer inspection revealed the person to be Pauline Rowell. It had begun to rain gently. In the faint beam of torchlight I tried in vain to examine my other companions, but all I could really make out were overcoats with hoods raised and dark silhouettes of umbrellas, shielding faces. Nobody spoke a word.

My eyes were becoming further accustomed to the near darkness as Pauline lead the way to the side of the road and we all climbed one by one over a stile, to continue walking some twenty metres along a narrow muddy footway. We came to some trees and then a small clearing. Pauline walked on, the thin, yellow torchlight dancing along unevenly flattened grass before her, and we followed until we came to a small, dark opening in the ground, about a metre square. Realizing we were about to climb down into this, I was concerned the light from Pauline's torch would be ineffective but I needn't have worried. It was enough for us to pick out some half a dozen stone steps.

We cautiously toed and felt our way down in single file and when my turn came I was surprised to find the palms of my hands, groping either side of me for balance, came into contact with the cool, smooth stones of a flint wall. As I reached the last step, I turned and was obliged to stoop down to enter through a faintly lit opening. I found myself standing in a small hallway, softly illuminated by one low voltage, electric light bulb. The walls, bar one, appeared to be made of compacted mud. This 'hallway' had a single large, heavy wooden door, grey with age, clad with iron, which stood open and through which we proceeded into a much larger room, brightly lit and furnished after a fashion in the gothic style with heavy oak table, chairs and wooden benches. The floor was stone but had been strewn with worn Persian rugs and several electric fan heaters hummed, turning on their pivots this way and that, warming the room. I heard the dull thump of the door as it was pushed back into place behind me and the clatter of the door-latch dropping home. I stared round at the bare walls and white-washed, coved ceiling – we were in what must have once been part of a crypt!

"Would you like a drink, Peter? Nothing alcoholic I'm afraid but I can offer coffee or cocoa." Frank made his way over to a small area which had been converted to a kitchen in the corner of the room.

I turned to look at the other people, now that there was sufficient light to do so. I didn't recognize either the man or woman and they looked quite ordinary and harmless – the type of people you would see in the supermarket on a Saturday morning, buying their weekly groceries. Frank hadn't waited for my reply but brought me a mug of steaming hot chocolate. I took it gratefully.

"This is Simon and Jenny Hopkins," he nodded to the couple. We all shook hands politely. "I'm afraid we've to wait a few minutes for the others. Make yourself comfortable, Peter." Frank went back to the kitchen area, followed by the other two and I then noticed for the first time that Pauline was no longer with us.

I sat down on one of the benches, leaning my back against the wall and sipping my drink. I assumed that Frank's wife was waiting to light the way for the other people expected. *Kelly would be with them*, I now thought, excitement quickening my pulse. The hot chocolate burned my mouth slightly but I continued to drink in an effort to calm the growing tension within me. I found myself thinking back to an early morning meeting in a shopping mall when Kelly and I had first begun to see each other seriously. Trancelike, I now remembered with vivid detail the events of that wonderful day.

We had arranged to meet near the sliding glass doors of the front entrance to the mall – I'd arrived slightly later than I'd intended and was wandering about aimlessly peering through the shop windows closest to the electronic doors when she appeared behind me wearing jeans and a baby-blue sweater, book bag slung over her shoulder, sunglasses perched atop her head. She smiled and on impulse I quickly, briefly, gathered her into my arms before releasing her just as suddenly. We strolled towards a coffee bar and sat for a while with steaming cappuccinos, talking about everything but the reason that we were there until I asked casually, "So what shall we do with our day?"

She had suggested a day by the sea and, as I had been preparing a unit of geography lessons on coastal erosion, I quickly agreed, thinking the trip might serve more than one purpose and give me the personal justification I was seeking for taking an unofficial day off work.

We purchased sandwiches and bottles of water and made our way to my mini, still chatting, except now the conversation was all about the coming day.

The weather had been a little dull when I'd set out that morning but the sun was now golden-bright and full of promise. We talked in the car, carefully questioning each other about the things we really wanted to know about our respective lives but without placing too much emphasis on the desire to know more.

The conversation continued after we arrived, as I parked the car in the gravel-surfaced parking lot provided for tourists and while we walked aimlessly along the grassy track to the ruin of an old roman church. After that we fell silent for a while. We peered up at what had been left of the towers then carefully made our way to the low iron fence, designed to keep people from walking too near the cliff edge, and looked down at the beach below. Perhaps feeling suddenly a little self-conscious and awkward, Kelly had kicked at a tuft of grass, until there was little more than mud left, with the heel of one of her flat shoes. I turned and sauntered on ahead, stopping a few steps on to turn and wait for her to catch me up and we wandered down the winding path to the beach, still a little shy in one another's company. We sat on the pebbles in the shelter of the groynes, which stood like short sentinels on either side of us, and leaned back on our elbows, idly tossing pebbles in the direction of the sea, though the water was some way out and they rattled harmlessly on the shingle.

Gradually, we began to talk hesitantly of the things we needed to say. Time rolled on like the ceaseless clouds across the blue, blue sky. The tide was coming in and we eventually clambered onto the huge grey hewn rocks, which had sometime been lifted by cranes to the beach to stop the eroding effect of the sea. We conversed endlessly about likes and dislikes, hopes and dreams and ate our sandwiches and drank our water. After a while we decided to continue our walk, further along the path above the beach that was hedged by marshy ground on the far side. We jumped down from the rocks and I hugged her to me and said possessively that she was with me and was all mine and I watched her flush with pleasure before taking her hand at last. We walked a mile or two, hand in hand, greeted by other pedestrians and the odd cyclist, all of whom smiled at us. It was as if the world was our own and we'd stepped out of time to be here together, undisturbed by any of the daily considerations of life.

All at once I was back in the crypt and the old feeling had returned. I felt alone, empty and frustrated. I wanted to feel Kelly's small frame in my arms and hold her close. I desperately wanted to know that she cared. I felt so achingly alone. *'Please come back to me,'* I silently prayed. *'Let it all be a silly misunderstanding. I want you. Oh God, I need you to want me. I will never ask anything of you but that you love me. Please, please come back'.*

"Peter." Frank stood before me, hand resting lightly on my arm, "Why don't you close your eyes for a while and rest? You've been staring into space for ages." He must have seen the tears threatening; I did feel very weary. "We'll wake you when it's time. Here's a cushion to rest your back more comfortably against the wall – I'm sorry there's nowhere you can lie down properly."

Drowsily, I did as I was told. The next thing I knew there was darkness, whispering and tiny specks of light dancing before my eyes.

'This time he will do it…'

I attempted to move but found I couldn't. I wanted to shout angrily but my voice emerged little more than a sob, "Where's Kelly?"

"I'm here, Peter. Give them the book."

"I can't see you. Where are you?"

"Give them the book, Darling. It will be alright."

"They can have the damned book I just want to see you. Why can't I move?"

'We haven't long….'
I wait for you. I long for you. How can you not now come?
Oh write to me, admit you care. Leave me not so alone.
I weep for you, cannot sleep, for you, cannot eat, will surely die.
You haunt my every waking thought. Please, do not mean 'goodbye'

With supreme effort I willed the darkness from my eyes and there she stood, smiling before me; my limbs were at once free from whatever unearthly embrace had held them and there was the dim, artificial light of the crypt and everyone standing around us, watching.

"Oh, Kelly, thank God…" I struggled to my feet and reached for her but Frank grasped my arm firmly.

"No, don't touch her, you fool," he warned. I tried to shrug him off angrily.
"Don't you ever learn? She'll shatter, man. Don't do it."

The words stopped me in my tracks and I stared, dumbstruck at my wife. She was smiling sadly and nodding. Wondering, I turned.

Frank had released his grip and was now sitting on the bench I had vacated, turning the pages of the poetry book.

"The answer must be here somewhere," he muttered.

I turned slowly back to face Kelly, gazing at her, comprehension dawning.

"It hasn't yet been written." I said the words quietly but the rustling of the pages ceased and I knew Frank was staring at my back.

"What?"

"The poem you are looking for. It hasn't been written yet."

"How can you possibly know that?"

"It's my desire for Kelly that brings her back, isn't it?" My question was rhetorical and I continued to gaze at Kelly.' "That book is like a passage, an emotional journey of a relationship. Wonder, admiration, hope, friendship, then unrequited longing. The poet falls into a mire of despair and self-loathing because he cannot progress any further – the object of his yearning doesn't see him or doesn't really acknowledge his existence anymore. The poem you are seeking hasn't been written because he still has to learn to live with this and allow the love to make the world shine for him, even though he can't expect fulfillment." All the while I looked at Kelly and she held my eyes, beseeching.

"Then we must find the poet and have him write the words…"

"That could prove difficult, Frank. He doesn't exist yet either."

I'd glanced briefly behind me to assure him that I knew what I was talking about, even though I wasn't really sure that I was right, and my eyes had left Kelly but a moment, yet when I looked back, the beautiful, compelling mirage of my wife had shimmered out of existence once more. There was a low murmur of sympathy from those gathered around me and I began to look from face to face, hurt

116

and bewildered. Others had joined the little group we had made on our arrival and there was now a veritable crowd of fourteen.

A flash of recollection suddenly took me back to the library and the group huddled at the far end of a room, faces turned briefly up to look in my direction, half hidden by shadows, before they hurried away. I now immediately recognized Kelly's former boyfriend, Tony, and then Marcia with several others from the youth drama group. Here was Gina, Katy and Scott – no wonder the faces had seemed familiar in the library! – And there were a couple of women, one in her mid twenties and another about my own age I surmised, neither of whom I knew. Yet the greatest surprise was Mark Chapman. I stared at him incredulously and he shrugged and had the decency to look embarrassed. He said simply, "I did say we'd have a lot in common!"

"How long have you been mixed up in all of this?"

It was as if only the two of us remained in the room. He stuck his hands in his trouser pockets, a familiar gesture I'd come to recognize as a sign that he was nervous and unsure of himself in a situation.

"Oh, I've been part of the group for some years. Sorry Pete, I couldn't tell you and you probably wouldn't have believed me about this anyway."

"What exactly is *this*?" And then as an afterthought, "Do you know my wife?"

At this point Frank intervened. "We'll explain everything all in good time, Peter. Try to be patient. I need to know what you meant in your last remark about the poet."

I allowed my eyes to stray to his without even bothering to try to disguise the contempt I was feeling. "Why do you suppose the greatest love stories end in tragedy?"

"Well some end happily…" I could see he was struggling to grasp my meaning.

117

"No, the truly great ones never end well. That's because in real life that kind of longing and passion can't last. You get to the mundane, everyday aspects of living and it melts away. When people first truly love like that, share each others' very souls – those who are lucky enough to experience it – they become God and Goddess in each other's eyes, perfection, everything dreamed of and desired. Sex can be spectacular – for a while – but eventually the heat dissipates and if they are lucky friendship remains." I wandered back over to the bench and sat back down. "Oh, I'm not saying lovers will not remain devoted to each other and want to spend the rest of their lives together but in the end the greatest love for most people is self-love. If it wasn't we would never survive as a race, we'd become extinct. That's why the greatest lovers, the real lovers can never be together."

"You sound so very cynical," Frank said dryly.

"No. I think I understand what he's getting at." Mark was staring at me with new respect. "A lot of people, when they lose their partners through death or divorce, suddenly burn with the intensity of that first love again. The pain triggers the remembrance of the God or Goddess and numbs the reality of humanity."

"That's ridiculous. Plenty of us love our partners just as much as when we first fell in love," broke in Pauline. I hadn't until then been aware that she had rejoined the group at last and I was, a little unkindly, amused at the annoyance in her voice.

There was an uncomfortable silence, a shuffling of feet. Perhaps those gathered were shocked by my theories and were trying to apply it to their own relationships and situations or maybe they too considered that perhaps Frank and Pauline had never really experienced that Grand Passion. Frank, on the other hand, seemed not in the least perturbed. I wondered whether it was because he had always subconsciously known the truth of what I'd said or was so busy thinking about the poetry book that it didn't occur to him to feel offended.

"I think I have the answer then." He snapped the book shut and handed it back to me with grim determination. "You, Peter, will have to write the poetry!"

"Now just a minute!" I protested. "I want to know what this is really all about. I'm not a poet, or circus animal that performs to your commands for that matter, and I don't see what poetry really has to do with all of this anyway."

I stood up again and began fretfully pacing up and down as my irritation, necessarily suppressed over the past few weeks, surged to the surface, maturing into a hard, cold fury. "I don't know how you have managed to convince me that I'm seeing my wife – I'm sure you have cameras rigged up somewhere or you've been drugging me or something. I don't know why you found it necessary to wreck my car and turn my house upside down and I have absolutely no idea how you managed to get in and redecorate my house then buy me a new car with 'my' signature. Frankly, I no longer care. I just want my peace of mind back. Either you know where Kelly is or you don't and if you want something from me for her safe return you'd better just tell me. I'll give it to you if I can, but let's stop these nightmarish mind games right now."

I expected something other than to see Frank with his head in his hands and Pauline on the verge of tears. Mark looked pale and badly shaken and, as I turned from one to the other of those present, it dawned on me that something was very wrong. Then Marcia stepped forward and gently touching my arm, gazed into my face as if willing me to believe her.

"Peter, we didn't do this. There are no cameras or tricks. We're simply trying to help get Kelly back – we've felt a certain responsibility for her situation – but from what you've just said there are obviously other people involved that we knew nothing about. Either that or it's an amazing coincidence that you should link those events with our connection to you. We had nothing to do with your house and car. We knew nothing about any of that. Why would you assume that we did?"

Chapter Thirteen

It took some seconds for her words to sink in and take effect and then I thought feverishly for precious moments to explain why I had believed them to be responsible. I knew it was not just the timing of events that had made me think that way and then I remembered. I took the book from the bench beside Frank.

"There was graffiti on my lounge wall; it was part of the sign on the bookshop door where Kelly told me I'd find this book. I think you'll agree it's a little too obvious to be pure coincidence."

There was a general muttering among those present. I looked about me now with renewed interest, searching for the tall stranger I had seen in the street the first time I experienced the vision of Kelly and then again as he emerged from my house after it had been set right; the person who'd stolen and returned my raincoat. He was not present.

"Well can someone please explain to me what's going on?"

"Kelly's on another plane of existence. I know that sounds ridiculous, insane even, but it's true." Mark spoke this time, his face earnest.

"We've all come to understand that there's more than just life and death as we commonly accept it. We've studied and shared our knowledge of religion, the paranormal and science in our search for understanding," Frank explained.

"Kelly was always very interested in the way strong emotions seemed to be involved in spiritual experiences." Pauline contributed now. "She suddenly became very interested in, and excited by, poetry, and she said that it was because of the way it seems to weave spells with language. Then one night she told us she'd discovered something really important and as soon as she was sure she would share it with us..."

"So what happened?"

"We don't know. We saw her once more at a meeting and she seemed preoccupied and unhappy, distant. She didn't want to talk. For a while we'd wondered if the two of you were having marital problems, and we didn't want to seem to be interfering by asking why she wasn't coming to the meetings. As a result we didn't see her again, not until a couple of times just recently, and then it was much in the same way as you saw her here tonight. When we told you we hadn't seen her for months and didn't know where she was when she went missing, we were completely sincere. By then we'd long since decided she'd simply lost interest in the group."

I couldn't blame them for that; I'd reached that very conclusion myself before she'd gone missing, yet I couldn't leave it at that. "But it's been so long..."

"When she last appeared to us she told us about the book and to go to the church to meet you. She doesn't find it easy to communicate; it seems to make her very weak."

"There was a letter. She wrote me a letter. How did she do that from another 'plane'?"

"She must have prepared in advance. She revealed where the letter was hidden and we posted it. I'm sorry Peter, that was my call," Frank lifted his head and I was uneasy to see anguish etched across his features. "I wish I had an easier explanation for you." He got up from his seat. "Look, there's nothing more we can do tonight. Will you please consider writing the poem? It's difficult to explain but I really believe Kelly feels that poetry is the answer."

122

I didn't reply at once and he didn't press me further. He simply said, "Listen, feel free to talk to any of us you wish and then I'll see you get back to your car safely. Perhaps you'd like another hot drink or something to eat? Anything we can do for you just let us know."

I wonder whether we aren't all the same in that we come to a place in our lives when we want to make something right but we just can't. We do or say something that can't be undone, or we don't do something that we should have, and once the moment has gone, we can't get it back and change the course of events that occur as a consequence. At such times we rely on others to forgive and if they don't we lose them forever. I did not wish this to be the case with Kelly.

I used to like watching situation comedies with Kelly, cosy on the sofa, her head on my shoulder, feet tucked up beside her. I would never have admitted to enjoying these shows and usually pretended smug contempt, agreeing to suffer watching simply to please her – ever the martyr. It wasn't that I thought they were particularly funny, although I admit to the occasional smile of acknowledgment at the honesty with which they portrayed common superficial, petty worries and concerns of humanity in the western world. What I really valued in such shows was the reassurance and comfort they provided as problems were always resolved, people always reached understandings and made things right; if only that could always be true of real life.

It is my conviction that it would be dreadful to reach old age, filled with regrets for opportunities that have been ignored and therefore missed, dreams unaccomplished. Most people at some time or other need a dream.

When I was ten, I decided I would become a famous actor. I would be so much more accomplished than those who trod the boards for the annual Christmas pantomimes and theatre productions to which my parents treated me, in London, Canterbury and the Medway towns, as a child. I never voiced my opinions but hugged them secretly to myself. Further, I inwardly scorned the skills of many of the performances in television drama. I was a quiet, introspective child – not really given to showing off – so the dream was doomed from the beginning. Of course, by the time I was a teenager I'd come to understand that what I'd perceived as weaknesses in the shows were actually professional ploys to draw the audience or viewer in, to create a sense of security in order to suspend belief. I had participated by becoming emotionally involved for a brief time in whatever story unfolded before my eyes, and so the actors and scriptwriters had done their jobs well. Yet I still believed I could do so much more.

By the time I went to university in my twenties such simple dramatic ambitions had been laid aside. I had come to the obvious conclusion that I wasn't really cut out for the attention and criticism accorded to actors as they worked. I knew there was fierce competition for work in the profession and it was not often a financially secure way of life. Most importantly, I hated the idea of constantly having to be someone other than myself and so I decided I would teach the art. Of course the idea had gradually evolved that I should one day write and direct an important play. I wanted to say something that would not just entertain but would impact on people's lives. With maturity, came the hard-won knowledge that I would need experience and to learn a great deal about drama, literature and the arts as a whole, before I could even attempt such a task. I decided that as soon as I had my degree in English and Drama, I would train to teach teenagers.

All went as planned until my first teaching practice in a tough urban comprehensive school, which almost killed any desire to teach whatsoever. I had little support from the Head teacher and staff at the place and, feeling a failure, I contacted the teaching college with a view to withdrawing from the program – giving up. I was called for interview with the Program Director and he took the time to convince me that I did, indeed, have what was required to succeed in teaching but that I should try the Primary stage. Two very different teaching placements rewarded the Director's faith in my abilities and I accepted that I did have a passion for teaching after all and couldn't just give it up. I told myself I could still be involved with drama and work outside of the school environment in my leisure time and there was always the notion of the great play I would one day write. I never gave up on my dreams.

Then Kelly came into my life and such fantasies became less urgent as I built my life with her. When she went missing, all my youthful aspirations ceased. My whole attention was taken up with the pain of loss as I was plagued with uncertainty and questions unanswered.

Now, if I was not mistaken in trusting these people, I was being presented with the opportunity, the motivation and even the material, not just to fulfill my destiny (if you'll forgive the dramatic phrase), but to recover all that I had lost. I had always enjoyed a challenge, yet now suddenly I was anxious that I was not equal to the task.

In a situation comedy this would be the part at which a supporting actor would give the protagonist a pep talk, thus providing the impetus for action, and everything would then fall neatly into place. So much for the silver screen! However, I couldn't fault the encouragement given and the faith that the members of the philosophy group appeared to have in my ability and I was caught up in the idea, deliberately refusing to acknowledge the absurdity of the situation. They were expecting me to write a very special poem for them, whereas I somehow comprehended it was not the poetry I should create but the poet!

I suppose it might have been easier for the younger members of the group to believe I could create a masterpiece because to them all things were still possible. To be fair, I had believed it myself at their age. With life experience, the more mature members (and I counted myself amongst these, despite only being in my early thirties while others were perhaps twice my age) had become a little more cynical, perhaps almost prophetic in expectancy. There seemed to be nothing 'new' to discover anymore – not in the arts anyway; all ideas seemed preconceived. Technology continued to develop but all that writers could hope to achieve would be to present the old universal truths in as new and refreshing light as possible, to give each generation the opportunity to learn to progress and evolve as human beings. Ahh, but wouldn't it be fantastic to discover or create that one, undreamed, completely original idea?

Anyway, to continue, the group did not stay very long in the crypt once I had made the decision to trust them and accept Frank's proposition (although I did not enlighten him about my theory that I should be writing a play rather than poetry). Apparently the crypt was an important place to meet for reasons appertaining to spiritual energy. I was cynical still but could not deny what had happened to me in front of fourteen or fifteen witnesses that night. However, I was relieved to discover, during the course of the evening, that few of them actually held strong beliefs in the supernatural. Nevertheless, like me, they were all prepared to accept the possibility of other dimensions in life that could not either be easily explained or understood. So there was no chanting of prayers or spells, no ceremonial conclusion to the evening; those gathered chatted amongst themselves for a while and gradually said their farewells and dispersed.

To my relief, I was not expected to be blindfolded on my return journey. All attempts at disguising the whereabouts of the crypt were now abandoned. Neither was I admonished with dire warnings concerning secrecy, nor even my integrity verbally invoked. My discretion was simply taken for granted and expected and I respected my new friends' confidence in me.

I left the poetry book in the crypt and followed the Rowells back to the Land Rover. The couple who had accompanied us on our outward journey left with Marcia and Tony. Mark tagged along with me and the Rowells and although we were silent pedestrians trudging back to the vehicle, we talked a great deal during the drive as we made our way back to Stillbury.

"Did you know Kelly before you met me?" I asked Mark, after a short discussion concerning the supernatural.

"I knew of her and saw her only once before tonight," he confessed. "I wasn't introduced to her as such and I doubt she has even registered my existence. She's a very beautiful woman."

"She's a very special person," Pauline interceded, "otherwise I don't believe she would be in the predicament she's in now."

"Yes – about that, what is all this 'vision' and 'shattering' business?"

126

"I take it you aren't a particularly religious man?" Mark queried.

"I'd like to say I've had my moments but not particularly, no," I replied dryly.

"How do you feel about sci-fi then? Think of the way many shows have their characters use electronic teleport systems. What you witnessed tonight is sort of similar – particle dispersal and re-organisation, I suppose. Except it isn't very stable and there doesn't appear to be any machinery involved."

"How is that possible?"

"Something or someone, perhaps even Kelly herself, has learnt to utilise the strength of her emotional psyche."

"Well, that's what we believe, anyway," this from Frank.

"She has such a love and zest for life but she wasn't happy," Pauline explained. I was about to protest but she added, "She loves you Peter, none of us doubt that, and we know you did your best for her, but you must have known she was depressed. She might not have said very much about the way she felt, yet her whole demeanor must have revealed her sadness to you as it did to us."

I had nothing to say to that, so it was fortunate that by this time we had reached our destination. I climbed out of the vehicle and watched as it growled and tumbled its way along the lane and out of sight. There were still so many questions to which I had no answers. I felt for the car key in my anorak pocket and made my way over to the Metro, parked on the grass verge near the church gate.

As I unlocked the door on the driver's side and the welcome light came on I noticed a piece of paper on the dashboard. I glanced round in the darkness, noting the glimmer of lights from far off, my ears sharpening to the drone of distant traffic on the dual carriageway, out of sight somewhere below the hill. The church was lit with spotlights and though in the shadows around the foot of the building ancient tombstones crouched like evil spectators waiting to pounce, I was quite certain not another living person was close by. I got into the car and reached for the paper with some apprehension. There were four words written on the note: '*Please bring Kelly home*'; there was nothing more but I recognised the slanting scrawl immediately with something akin to fear – it was from the hand of Maureen Butler.

Chapter Fourteen

I was going to be late for work yet again. I'd overslept and when I finally did come to, aware of the tinny music from my clock radio, I hurriedly pulled on some clothes and grabbed my brief case. Then, rushing from the house to the car, I noted, with some trepidation, the Metro had a flat tyre. *It was history repeating itself – an improbability in the world of fiction but only too possible in the real world*, I thought. There wasn't time to walk to school and when I flipped open my mobile to contact the school secretary I merely reached the answering machine. I didn't leave a message but hastily thumbed the number for April's mobile instead; she answered on the second ring. Fortunately she was just about to get into her car so was willing to make a short detour to collect me on her own way to work.

April was eager to know all that had happened concerning my meeting with Frank and I filled her in on the events of the previous evening. She listened quietly without interrupting and there was a brief silence when I'd finished, before she spoke.

"Kelly was really there for a while? Not some sort of illusion?"

"She was there and as real as you and me." I was relieved that April seemed to accept this without too much concern.

"Do you think one of the group members put the note in the car?"

"Why would they do that? They could have just given it to me."

"Was the car locked?"

I thought for a moment before nodding; I could see what she was getting at.

"It must have been the person who acquired the car on your behalf. They have a spare set of keys."

"You think Maureen purchased the car? She's dead, April. I've spoken to my father-in-law and read the obituary. I didn't go to the funeral but I'm pretty sure she's gone."

The message from Kelly's father, informing me of Maureen's death, had come two days after my call to him when I'd first learnt about her accident. The news had been a shock but I had been too preoccupied with my own concerns to dwell very much on it. I'd returned his call but he hadn't wanted to talk for long and he hadn't accepted my offer to visit him; I'd been selfishly grateful and done nothing more. I knew he had family close by and friends to support and help him through it all and I didn't feel at that time I could cope with the emotional drain of fresh loss. I was fond of Maureen and there would be time for remorse and sorrow later.

I was half expecting April to remind me of the strange evening when I'd had a lift from the supposedly unconscious woman. Instead my friend was more practical, "Perhaps she wrote it some time ago, like Kelly and her letter."

"I think you're probably right but somebody still put this note in the car and they had to have a reason. I mean, of course I am going to do everything in my power to get Kelly back. I didn't need to be asked."

"We should find the mysterious detective guy. I would bet you next month's salary, he holds the key to the mystery and possibly keys to your car and house too!" She drew up outside the school gate, pulling hard on the car hand-break. "Let's have supper at my place tonight and we'll talk some more. I have a surprise for you anyway."

I thanked her for the lift and hurried into school glad to be there just before the bell rang for first lesson.

At break time I caught Mark's eye and he raised his eyebrows in acknowledgement but made no attempt to join me, choosing instead to continue his conversation with Caroline. She, on the other hand, half turned to see who Mark had greeted and stopped talking mid-flow, lightly touching his arm for a second before coming over to where I stood near the tea urn.

"I was just telling Mark, my Decree Absolute came through this morning. I'm sad, of course, but relieved too. How would you feel about joining us for a quick drink by way of celebration after school?"

"Er, thanks Caroline but I already have plans. Congratulations though," I kissed her face then smiled knowingly back at Mark. "Besides, I think three's a crowd." Caroline reddened perceptibly and giggled, pretending to push me away, while glancing surreptitiously back at her former companion.

"Ok, your loss …"

I excused myself and took my mobile telephone from my pocket to text April my thanks for her help that morning, together with the invitation, and enquiring whether she would like me to stop off for fish and chips on the way to her place. She responded almost immediately, telling me not to worry she already had everything under control.

She did indeed have everything under control; when I knocked at her front door early that evening an extraordinarily attractive blonde invited me into the house, introducing herself as Allie, April's best friend. This perplexed me a little since I had considered myself to hold that position in April's affections, but I said nothing, smiling quietly and shaking hands. The dining table was already set and steaming dishes of chilli, rice and a basket of sliced, home-made bread graced the centre. April joined us from the kitchen, carrying a bottle of Cabinet Shiraz and wine glasses.

The evening was panning out well; Allie was interested in everything about school and education and listened attentively when her questions were answered. She never did reveal anything about her own profession or career and I was a little surprised when, soon after we had finished the meal, Allie got up to leave, saying she needed to be back in London before midnight. She once again shook my hand warmly, smiling into my eyes, and then kissed April affectionately before letting herself out of the house. April didn't even see her to the door. I gazed at my friend for a while, mystified. She in turn was staring at the tablecloth, twiddling the stem of her wine glass between her finger and thumb, as if her mind was a million miles away. Eventually she spoke without looking up.

"She didn't have much to say about herself did she?"

"Well, now you come to mention it, no. Very nice women, though. Is she the one…?"

April looked up and smiled sadly. "Yes, well, no. She helped me sort myself out actually, last night. Have some more wine," she effortlessly uncorked a third bottle and deftly filled my glass and her own before I even had time to protest. "I insist. You'll need it." She got up and went over to the sofa, took a long drink from her glass and set it on the coffee table. I sat down by her side, waiting, the wine she'd poured for me untouched.

"Do you know, I've never really cried over anybody before, never felt that deeply involved, but last night I didn't think I would ever be able to stop my tears and she just held me in her arms and rocked me to and fro until I couldn't cry anymore?"

"What did she say to make you cry?" I could hardly believe what I was hearing, April cry? Never in a million years…

April continued as if I hadn't spoken, "It was quite easy for me to come out you know. Nobody was shocked or threatened to disown me. That's the awful thing."

"April, you're worrying me a bit now. Why don't you just tell me what happened."

"I don't know if I can." She leaned forward, resting her elbows on her knees and I glimpsed a look of intense misery on her face before she covered it with her hands. I instinctively moved forward to comfort her and she didn't resist. "Oh God help me, Peter, I do love you so." Her voice was muffled by my jacket but I could tell she was distressed and weeping again.

"I love you too, kid, and I'm here for you – you know that – so tell me what the problem is. Maybe I can help."

"I just did. I love you. Not Allie. Not another woman. You. It's you I love. It always has been but I just couldn't admit it before, even to myself."

I didn't know what to do. I just sat there, tense and unmoving, with her resting against my shoulder sobbing quietly. I was suddenly uncomfortably aware of her warm breath on my neck. I felt absolutely stunned.

"Well, say something." She moved out of my embrace and peered up at me, tear-streaked face, enquiring eyes.

I looked away, hanging my head and I actually found myself wringing my hands. "April, I can't, I don't, I mean…"

"I know. Kelly. It's okay. That's why I'm going to help you to get her back."

"You are?" I felt I'd wandered into some strange dream where everything was turning upside down and inside out, but then life had been a bit like that recently.

"Of course." She put her arm round my shoulders and kissed my hair. "No point in us both being miserable, now, is there? Finish your wine I have something to show you." She went over to the lounge cabinet and opened the same drawer through which she had searched for the poetry book. This time she brought back a quite different text. It was a modern paperback entitled *Handwriting and all it reveals.* It appeared she had Maureen's note in mind and I understood that, but failed to see how the book could help. It was one of those guides, written by an expert, explaining the significance of the way in which people formed letters, the gist being that various shapes and styles exposed the personality/character traits of the writer. April quickly reassured me that there was a chapter on how to compare pieces of writing to see whether they had been composed by the same person. I pointed out that I had nothing with which to compare Maureen's note and that I had just recognised her hand, and then I felt immediate remorse as I saw the enthusiasm die on April's face.

"I'll take the book with me and have a read anyway," I said quickly. "You never know, there might be something I haven't considered." I think she knew I was trying to be kind but she visibly brightened anyway. Selfishly, I wondered whether she would be as useful and astute in my quest to get Kelly back now, or whether her emotions would somehow have a dampening effect on her generally sharp intellect. I pushed the thought away as I bid her goodnight with genuine humble appreciation that she should have been so honest with me. Yet on my way home I couldn't help but consider whether April's infatuation, for I genuinely believed it could be nothing more than that, would be detrimental to our friendship.

As it turned out, it actually helped matters. I didn't sleep well that night, tossing and turning, replaying the scene in my head again and again to see if I could have or whether I should have said or done anything differently, until at last, succumbing to troubled but heavy exhaustion an idea dropped into my consciousness; it went from freefalling to spinning more sedately, like a sycamore seed riding a breeze. Eventually it settled in my mind, clear and solid as I re-emerged into full wakefulness again. A few seconds and I sat up abruptly and sprang from my bed in the grey light of dawn, snatching up my glasses and hurrying to find paper and a pen. First the poem, questioning the unrequited passion of another:

If

If fantasies were summer breezes drifting out to sea,
Watched from a solid rock of friendship, shaped by trust,
And confidences, shared with ease, set my sadness free,
I'd surrender all anxieties and give in to pure lust.
If loving dreams sang through trees, away from worldly fears,
While ferns sheltered warm caresses wrapped in deep affection,
And breathless peace with passion kissed away uncertain tears,
I'd take your hand and follow you and would not fear rejection.
If just a smile, a touch, a word could set my soul on fire,
While gentle kisses eased my pain and filled my heart with truth,
And I felt safety in your arms expressing my desires,
I'd know our lives would not be harmed, if I made love with you.

Where did the poem come from? I suppose I'd been remembering the excitement, passion and sheer pleasure culminating in a sense of real peace and fulfillment when I first spent time romantically with Kelly on some clandestine excursion, to the coast or picnicking deep in some leafy woods. Then, half-asleep and still vaguely worried about April, I'd wondered what it would be like to have a 'fling', to become briefly involved, just to be able to experience the contentment of being loved again. My sex-drive had been dormant for so long I suppose I hadn't acknowledged the inescapable truth that it was still there, the desire to express physical and emotional needs. I swallowed a sudden surge of bitter loneliness, refusing hardly to acknowledge it; there was much to do.

Chapter Fifteen

Scene 1 – The stage is set up to look like a fast food restaurant. Two young women sit at a table near the window, chatting, their attention absorbed by a man in his mid to late thirties seated alone at a table to one side of them.

Joan: I'm sure that's him. He lives quite near us. Have you read the novel?

Annette: No. I'll have to get a copy.

Joan: I have it with me, just a moment, (*rummages in her bag.)* Ah, this is it. Listen.

She leans towards her companion to read, their heads almost touching in their eagerness to share the contents of the book.

Joan: He met her in the city on a Management training course whilst already in a relationship with a nurse. He knew she was out of his league – she was gorgeous, smart and well-heeled – but for some inexplicable reason she encouraged his attentions and he was delighted when she not only agreed to a relationship with him but also later accepted his impulsive proposal of marriage. He was completely, utterly smitten.

They bought an apartment on Canary Wharf, pleased to be part of the fashionable set. Then, a month into the marriage, she left him for a work colleague and he was dealt the final devastating blow to his self-esteem when she admitted she had been unfaithful for the entire duration of their relationship and into their marriage. He lost his trendy home, along with most of his financial assets, and he thought he would die of misery. Some say love is simply a mixing of chemicals and electrical impulses in the brain, designed by nature to ensure the continuation of the human species. One thing was for sure, regardless of whatever cocktail had swamped his grey matter, this man was certain he had never felt that way before and he would never allow himself to become so deeply involved again.

Annette: Bit bleak, isn't it?

Joan: Yeah, but that's what I'm saying, it's exactly what happened!

A woman enters the restaurant, looks around and sees the man who has raised a hand to attract her attention. She joins him.

Man: Coffee?

Woman: Yes please, plenty of sugar as usual. How are you?

In the background Joan leans forward and addresses Annette in a stage whisper:

Joan: I think that's his second wife. I've seen them together a couple of times.

Man: I've just been tuning in on a couple of my literary critics

He inclines his head towards the two women by the window

Woman: Critics? Those two? They're more like fans. It's quite nice to be thought your wife, though, I have to say.

She smiles in acknowledgment of them and they give a little wave and huddle closer over the book. The man fetches coffee for the woman and sits back down, handing her two small sachets of sugar. She proceeds to empty them one at a time into the hot drink.

Man: They're quite wrong you know. I didn't lose the apartment, I bought her out but sold it eventually when I met and married Sandra. She did more or less ruin me financially though.

Woman: Ben, you need to let it go. I thought the book was supposed to be cathartic.

Man: My message upset you, didn't it?

Woman: Yes, I can't lie to you, it did. It's just that I thought you trusted me. I believed we felt the same.

Man: I never lied to you.

Woman: Except by omission – the worse type of lie. That's what I've come to tell you. I think the world of you, you know that.

Man: But…

Woman: I'll never be able to trust you again, not if you can't trust me. You seem to have no concept of how much you've hurt me. I believed we'd go on this way for the rest of our lives. Now I realise how naive I've been, living in a fantasy world where nobody would get hurt.

Man: (*irritably*) I don't like it when you become so intense.

The woman pushes the coffee away from her, untouched, and stands.

Woman: I know. That's another reason why I think it would be best for both of us if we just leave it there. Goodbye Ben.

She leaves the restaurant, head held high, without looking back. Joan and Annette watch her leave then approach the man.

Annette: Excuse me, Sir. Would you sign our book?

Man: (*his eyes still on the door as it closes behind the retreating* *woman)* I'm sorry, not right now. Maybe some other time. *He gets up and leaves.*

Scene 2 – A kitchen.
Ben leans against the sink looking at a mobile telephone. The back door opens and a woman enters carrying various shopping bags. She closes the door with her foot. Ben glances up briefly then goes back to gazing at his phone.

Ben: So. What's all that lot then?

Sandra: Oh, just a few things from the sales. They were really cheap.

She puts the bags down and tries to slide them out of sight with her foot.

Sandra: Who are you texting?

Ben: Nobody, I was checking my messages to see if there was anything from work.
He puts the phone in his pocket

Sandra: Let me see.

Ben: What? No. Why?

Sandra: There were numbers I didn't recognise on the bill again. I want to know what you are hiding.

Ben: I'm not hiding anything. Unlike you. How much have you spent this time?

She shrinks back.

Sandra: Not much. I just want to look nice for you, that's all. I don't want you to be tempted by … anyone else. I don't know what the fuss is all about; you've just had a book published!

Ben: (*exasperated*) I don't get anything back from that for months yet. It's not like a bestseller you know. I'm with a small, barely known publisher and they have to cover costs for getting it out there in the bookshops. Then the agent will take his share. You can't go spending money we haven't got.

Sandra: (*cajoling*) I've found something to spice up our lovemaking, for you and me tonight. Do you want to come and see?

Ben: What, after you've been accusing me of God knows what? Forget it.

Sandra: Ben, please. I didn't mean anything. I love you so much. Please let's just go to bed and make up.

Ben: I'm not interested, I tell you. Leave me alone. *He storms from the house, slamming the door.*

Sandra takes a mobile telephone from her own coat pocket. She keys in a number then puts the phone to her ear.

Sandra: James, I'm sorry to bother you but I've changed my mind; do you still fancy going for that drink with me? *Pause* Well, you were right, where's the harm in having a drink with a friend? Actually, I could really do with a shoulder to cry on and Ella's out of town. Please, I would be so grateful.

***

I took a sip of coffee and set my mug back down by the computer keyboard, peering at the monitor with a sense of satisfaction. (For once the machine was working perfectly and didn't hamper my creative flow in any way.) I wondered whether Caroline would recognise herself if she ever saw the play. I didn't think she would since James (a.k.a. yours truly, modestly taking the forename of Fleming's famous fictitious spy, 007) would help her sort everything out with her husband – not at all like real life.

I mused for a while longer, thinking about the lovers, Ben and Ella, wondering from whence they had sprung. I couldn't think of anyone remotely like them and yet they seemed so real while I was writing; I could almost feel the raw emotions in their relationship. I continued tapping away at my keyboard, surprised and exhilarated at the rate at which the play grew and took shape.

An hour or so later, I was surprised to hear the front-door bell; it was still early – not yet 7 o'clock. I pulled on a dressing gown and went downstairs to investigate. It was, of course, April. I opened the door wide and stood aside to allow her entry, then went to the kitchen to make fresh coffee. She closed the front door and followed me, seating herself at my little kitchen table without a word. The silence between us continued and then stretched on awkwardly, so I decided to break it and vanquish the unspoken anxieties that could ruin the friendship forever.

"I've been writing. I think I have the play we need. I've even penned a poem of sorts, not *the* poem, of course, that's for the character in the play to do. My poem's a bit of an anomaly at present because it isn't in any way linked to the play. I'd appreciate your opinion on what I've done so far. Maybe you could suggest some improvements…" I was aware that I was rattling on nervously so I stopped.

"Have you forgotten school?"

I glanced at the kitchen clock, swearing under my breath.

"You go get ready. I'll tidy up down here. It doesn't look as if you've washed up in days!"

"I've hardly been here," I yelled back as I took the stairs, two at a time.

Once again April drove me to school; I'd had no time to do anything about the flat tyre on my own car. She promised to read over my work that evening. It was decided we would have supper together again, this time in my newly tidied kitchen.

The day passed uneventfully enough and, as foreseen by the pair of us, the evening found April upstairs, engrossed in the words on

142

the computer screen, while I prepared lamb chops with a rosemary and honey glaze.

After a while she wandered into the kitchen. I was draining the potatoes.

"It doesn't feel right, Ben and Sandra getting back together. The James bloke isn't very convincing either…"

"Oh, tell it like it is – why don't you – don't spare my feelings!"

She ignored my attempt at humorous sarcasm. "Maybe Sandra and James could get together, that might work."

"Definitely not! Anyway, I thought you said he wasn't very convincing. Maybe I should just scrap him and think of something else."

She stared, obviously baffled at my reluctance to use her suggestion. "No, no, I didn't mean he didn't seem real, I just don't see why he'd be so accommodating and helpful in advising Sandra about marriage. She's an attractive woman; surely he would be looking after his own interests…"

"Not necessarily. Maybe he's just a nice bloke. Why are women always so fascinated and infatuated by self-centered, moody men like Ben?"

April wasn't quite as quick to hide her amusement as she'd thought she'd been and seemed surprised when I shot her a dark look.

"Well, some women like a bit of mystery, especially if it concerns emotional pain. It brings out the nurturing instinct. They want to make everything better."

"Hmm. I know of one or two males who can be like that too; perhaps the sexes aren't so very different after all. Hey, I've got it! He wants to help because he saw his own parents' marriage break down and knew what the consequences would be for the children."

"So Sandra and Ben have children?"

"Er, no. Hmm, that's another idea blown out of the window then." I proceeded to ladle food onto plates.

"You could invent some. You don't have to see them on stage, just put in the odd sentence about them."

"No. Ben doesn't want children. In fact, he can't have them."

"Really? How's that?"

"Vasectomy."

"I don't recall reading that. Is he based on you then?"

I'd just taken a gulp of water and almost choked, "Good Heavens, No! Whatever made you think I've had a vasectomy? Do you really think Ben is anything at all like me?"

April shrugged. "I just thought, being the protagonist and all… Anyway, I really think Ben and Ella ought to be together. They're so obviously meant for each other. You had me in tears when she left."

"That's the whole point. Their love doesn't fade because they never have the opportunity to grow tired of each other. They never lose the sexual tension and yearning that drew them together again and again. She had to leave for his sake because she knew he could never be happy if he betrayed his wife by abandoning her."

"It's a bit like the doctor in Coward's *Brief Encounter*, then. I see. That makes sense."

"Well," I set our plates of food on the table and fished in the kitchen drawer for cutlery, "there are obviously a few problems to iron out and I think we need someone unbiased to give us a few pointers."

April didn't argue but pulled a face and took up her mug of tea, colouring slightly and trying not to squirm in her seat. "Who did you have in mind?" I flipped the tea-towel I'd been drying my hands on, across my shoulder and took a card from the windowsill where it had been laying since I'd received it. I passed it to April. She read it and frowned. "Abigail Maitland. You're thinking of taking the play to a book club meeting?"

I sighed, took the card back and sat down to my meal. "Have some imagination, April. I was just thinking of asking the woman to look at the play and give me her opinion. She reads a great deal and seems very knowledgeable about literature generally and she might have a few ideas."

"Well, I suppose it couldn't hurt. You told me you've only met her and spoken on the telephone once. What made you think of her?"

I shrugged, "Instinct, I suppose." My attention was taken up for a moment cutting up my chop and forking meat into my mouth. I had no intention of explaining about my strange dream in which dogs had appeared as children and my need to follow Kelly's advice to consider my dreams carefully. For some reason it seemed too personal to share, even with April. I chewed thoughtfully for a moment then swallowed. "Look, we've only got until Friday before Autumn break." We can call on Abigail together then, Okay?" She nodded and I changed the subject. "By the way, what's the latest news at school? Have you got the results from the OFSTED inspection yet?"

***

That night I dreamed of Ben and Ella. They were sitting on a bench near a lake in the beautiful garden I'd visited in earlier dreams. Ella was weeping uncontrollably and Ben had his arm about her shoulders, talking in a soothing tone but the words seemed to hold little comfort for the woman.

"All this hesitating has to stop. We can't go on like this. You know I want you."

145

"I can't do this anymore, Ben. I can't keep coming between you and your wife. Please understand. It's no good. I have to go away."

"I don't want you to go. I do trust you, woman. I know you think I don't but I do. I want to spend the rest of my life with you. I think about you all the time and I get worried someone will notice because I'm so distracted. But now I think, so what if they do notice? It will bring everything out into the open. If that isn't love I don't know what is."

"It's just a fantasy, Ben. See,"

I watched as she pulled away from him slightly, and felt inside her jacket pocket. She pulled out a piece of paper which she unfolded and held out for him to read.

"I wrote this for you. Perhaps it will help you to understand."

Ben cast a cursory glance at the paper then dismissed it. "I don't want to read it. I don't want to understand. I don't even like poetry.

"Oh how *can* you say that?"

"Look, just go away if you must. I'm not arguing anymore. If this is Goodbye, so be it. I have to go."

I could see he was angry as he strode off. Ella sat head bowed, her sobs wracking her whole body. The piece of paper dropped from her hand and a breeze brought it to my feet. I picked it up and scanned the writing. It was the poem I had composed that very morning.

Chapter Sixteen

The confirmation that I was, in fact, dreaming vividly almost roused me from my slumber. However, I didn't allow myself to wake. Instead I made a conscious decision to use this opportunity to assist me in my writing. I approached Ella.

"Excuse me; I think this belongs to you."

She glanced up then reached up to take the paper from my hand, muttering her thanks, awkwardly brushing her tears from her face. Uninvited, I sat down beside her.

"I hope you don't think I'm intruding but that poem – it's very good. You seem to have a natural talent for writing. *Well, it was my dream so why shouldn't I flatter myself?*

"I suppose you saw us arguing. You must think I'm an idiot."

"No, I don't think that at all. From what I could see you've every reason to be upset. Would you like to talk about it? I know you don't know me but sometimes it can help to confide in a stranger – someone you're unlikely ever to meet again. I don't live in these parts so you see you'd be quite safe telling me anything you want to."

She stared at the ground for a moment and I watched her profile in silence. I marvelled at the detail of my dream; I could see each individual hair that made up the curls on her head, so vivid was this vision. I also noted weary lines of tiredness about her eyes. She nodded slowly yet seemed reluctant to begin so I took the lead.

"Have you known each other long?"

"Forever, since before he was married. You must be appalled that I could be involved with a married man, except, well it wasn't really like that. Not at first anyway. We were," she hesitated, "friends I suppose." She glanced at me but I made no comment and gave not the slightest indication of judgmental opinion. In fact, I concentrated hard on appearing sympathetic and her swift appraisal of my facial expression seemed to reassure her, so she continued.

"I met him through a mutual acquaintance just after his divorce and he became part of my circle of friends. Everyone thought he was great except me. I didn't really like him much because he made some pretty harsh comments to different people in the group; he didn't seem to care about other people's feelings but the others thought it hilarious, so long as they weren't on the receiving end." She paused, sighing. I waited for her to go on.

"Anyway, one night we were at someone's house and Ben had been drinking quite a bit. The others decided to go and get some food from a nearby Indian restaurant, leaving him sprawled in an armchair and I was left to get plates ready, set the table, that sort of thing. I ignored him until he suddenly made some caustic comment about how I had the perfect life. I don't know why I allowed it to get under my skin and irritate me so much but I found myself telling him just how 'perfect' my life had been so far. I lost my parents when I was ten, you see. Anyway, we started talking about really personal things – I guess it was the alcohol loosening his tongue – although to be fair to him when the others returned he went quiet again. Every now and then during the course of the evening I looked over at him and caught him watching me intently. In the months that followed, he'd sometimes call round my flat for a drink and chat by himself. I began to like and respect him and I know it was mutual. I never met his first wife but I know he was really devastated by the divorce; he seemed brittle emotionally, glassy almost. Yet he really could be quite nasty in a funny sort of way – can you understand what I mean?"

"Your friendship deepened though?"

She hardly needed the encouragement, fervently launching into an explanation as if trying to justify the way she had behaved to a court of appeal and convince them that she was innocent; although gradually she admitted she was as much at fault as he was for the way things developed.

"Yes, our friendship became quite important to both of us over the years. I was there when he met Sandra, his second wife, and I went to their wedding. I work with Sandra, you see, and I introduced them. She never really minded that we were friends but after a while we stopped telling her that we still occasionally met for coffee and the odd walk in the park. I don't know why. Then he started talking about them having problems. I think he was trying to understand the feminine perspective by discussing things with me."

She blew her nose on a tiny lace handkerchief. "The trouble is he started to compare Sandra and me. I tried to dissuade him at first but I was vulnerable. I'd suffered a broken relationship myself by then and the truth is I wanted to become closer, more intimate. Then he started to talk about taking things further. He wants us to become lovers, to find a place of our own."

"But you don't want that?"

"I do. I really do. I just don't think he's really in love with me and I'm not prepared to break up his marriage for less."

"Why do you say he doesn't love you? He looked pretty sincere to me."

"He doesn't trust me. He says he does but he doesn't, not really. I asked him after I read his book – it's loosely based on his first marriage except he turned it into a crime thriller, a detective novel."

"Really, did he murder his wife in the book then?"

"No." She smiled weakly and sniffed. "He rescued her from

impending doom and made her rich."

"That was very generous. Were you jealous then?"

"No. In real life I think she lives in the North and is remarried, not much of a threat to anyone. I doubt she even knows about his novel. After I'd read it I asked him whether he was still in love with her and he wouldn't give me a straight answer. Then he said something like, 'Well you've read the opening paragraphs of my book, you of all people should know I can't love or trust anyone in quite the same way ever again.' Then he tried to soften the blow by saying that I was special to him in a way nobody else would ever be and that he did love me very much, enough to want to be with me for the rest of our lives. You're a man. Why do you suppose, if he isn't in love with me, that he would want to be with me?"

I shrugged, "Companionship, sex."

"But he could get those from Sandra."

"Yes but I suspect you understand him better and are more patient so he prefers to be with you."

"Well it isn't enough. So I've tried to end it. You saw what happened. I suppose I deserve to suffer, don't I?"

"Do you really want to know what I think?"

She nodded, watching me.

"I think you will walk away from this and start a new life somewhere else. What's more, you will meet and marry someone free to love you the way you deserve to be loved."

She smiled gratefully. "I don't think so. I don't think I can ever feel quite the same again, although you're very kind to say so. Are you married?"

"Er, yes. Ironically, my wife has left me and I'm trying to get her back."

"I'm so sorry!" I was touched at the way she reached for my hand and I could actually feel the cool pressure of her palm against my skin. "You've been so good listening to me. Do you need someone to talk to?"

"No. Thanks. You've already helped me more than you can ever know. Don't worry about Ben. He does love his wife in his own way and you're right, he would only be wretched if he betrayed her by leaving. Then he'd end up resenting you." I gently slid my hand from beneath hers and rose from the seat. "If you are strong and leave now you'll never really lose his love and, what's more, one day he'll come to appreciate just how strong you've been and the sacrifice you've made for him." I smiled down at her. "You only really think you'll never feel the same about anyone else because you believe you love him as much as he loved his ex-wife. He said that he could never love anybody else, didn't he? But it doesn't have to be that way. Do the right thing, Ella." I smiled solemnly down at her. "I have to go now. Be good. I promise everything will be okay."

"Good luck with your marriage," she called after me and I felt myself slowly coming out of sleep into wakefulness.

I stared into the darkness for a while, reliving the scene. It had seemed so real, so much so in fact that I felt quite melancholy. Once again I found myself observing the light gradually filter into my room through the curtains announcing another dawn. An errant blackbird pierced the early morning quiet with a single melodic enquiry and then fell silent again when there was no response. I turned back onto my side and went back to sleep.

***

"I have to be honest with you, Peter, your play's a little ... what can I say? It's rather different to the sort of entertainment people are generally interested in these days." She looked up sharply, "Please don't feed Trottwood; she has problems with her weight."

April guiltily placed the remains of the biscuit on her saucer and put her cup of tea down onto the coffee table. The spaniel eyed her balefully, not moving a centimetre from her position near April's feet. Abigail heaved herself out of her armchair and went to the patio doors behind us, calling to both dogs to let them out into the garden.

"People seem to want lots of action, sex, violence, that type of thing but your play is quite uneventful."

"Boring?" I supplied dispiritedly.

"Not boring, exactly. I just couldn't quite make out the point of the play. Are you hoping to stage it?"

"That *is* what usually happens with plays," April interjected. "I think you're being too critical. It's a sensitive reflection on relationships in modern society. I'm a drama teacher so I should know," she finished triumphantly.

I shot a warning look at my friend but she stuck her chin out defiantly. However, Abigail was not in the least offended.

"On the contrary, I think it's exactly right for the stage. It is, as you say, both sensitive and thought provoking, I just wondered what you were trying to tell the audience is all. I wasn't really criticising."

"Surely it's an obvious call for a return to good old-fashioned values and a criticism of the lack of morality today." April was obviously in an argumentative mood.

Abigail raised her eyebrows, considered April's confident appraisal for a moment and then inclined her head in acquiescence.

"Actually, I dreamed up the two main characters in my sleep. They seemed to have a particularly strong emotional bond and I wanted to see what would happen. The play sort of wrote itself. Sorry, I know that doesn't sound particularly artistic." (This last comment was addressed to April.)

"On the contrary, many writers claim their characters have a life of their own. In fact the French novelist, Emile Zola, wrote a series of novels he believed could be examined as a social experiment. He created characters which he placed in particular circumstances so that he could discover how they would 'behave' or 'evolve' as people."

"So do you think the play will work?"

"Well I think you might need to tweak the writing here and there, nothing major, and that will come as you direct it. Yes, I think it has a very good chance of success. It will probably appeal to the older generation, of course, and you might consider setting it in a different time period, make it more nostalgic perhaps."

"I don't think I had any particular period in mind when I wrote it." I replied, frowning.

"You have mobile telephones in Scene 2 – they're a relatively modern commodity."

"Ha, I see what you mean! Funny, I kind of felt it to have taken place several decades ago, although that again might be the old-fashioned values shining through. Yes I believe you could have something there. I'll have to think about it, see what needs altering. Thanks Abigail, you've been a great help."

"It was a pleasure to read, Peter. I hope you are being sincere in telling me I have been of some assistance. It would be such a shame if you just became pessimistic and shelved the project because of my humble opinion. Now," she was at once more business-like, "how do you feel about bringing your girlfriend along to the next book club evening?"

I promised to think about it without even bothering to correct her assumption concerning my relationship with April. The latter sat in the passenger seat of the Metro, shuffling through the sheaf of papers, which made up the only hard copy of my play in existence, as I started the engine.

"Peter, when did you add this part?" She was looking at the conversation between Ella and the stranger. "I don't remember reading it before. It makes the world of difference and I think you might be wrong about the poem. It makes sense now and it may actually be the one we're looking for."

"We?" I grinned knowingly. "Since when did you become part of Kelly's group? Does that mean you're coming to the next meeting then? It's scheduled for tomorrow."

"Just try keeping me away!"

"I was hoping you'd say that. Now, I think we are going to that new Italian restaurant in town for lunch and afterwards back to my place to listen to some music and relax." She gave me the oddest, speculative look but said nothing and I took her silence as approval.

The meal was excellent. We agreed not to talk about the play, the meeting, or the past, but instead discussed art and the latest music and fashions. She laughed about the clothes some of her students wore then said she'd appreciate my opinion on a dress she'd seen in a nearby boutique window. After settling the bill, I was literally dragged along by my arm to see the manikin displaying the garment in the shop window. Fortunately once I'd expressed my approval she did not insist I go inside the store. We just went back to the car and I drove to my house. I asked her to wait in the car while I collected a handful of Compact Discs. She frowned questioningly when I returned, noting the overnight bag and checking through the selection of classical music I had chosen, when I placed the CDs on her lap.

"I thought I'd stay at your place tonight, if you don't mind. I'll bunk on your sofa again – I don't seem to have such vivid dreams there and it will save time tomorrow if I don't have to pick you up first." I fixed my eyes on the road, unable to look at her, almost afraid to breathe in case I gave myself away.

April seemed completely oblivious and agreed without hesitation. "Ok, that makes sense. I still have some of that chardonnay left if

154

you're interested."

"Even better."

Chapter Seventeen

"April, those savories were delicious – I didn't think I'd be able to eat anything else after that meal this afternoon but they were a treat. The wine's greatly appreciated too and the film really took my mind off things. Thanks."

"Any time, Partner.' She held her hand up and attempted to high five me – we were both slightly inebriated by this time – we missed each others' raised palms by about a metre then fell to giggling. She stood up. "There's more wine if you want to refill the glasses and put some of that music on that you brought. You aren't tired yet, are you?"

"Not at all. Just pleasantly relaxed."

"Good. I won't be long."

She left the room to go upstairs and I quickly did as she had requested, settling easily onto the thick piled carpet with my back against the sofa, another glass of wine in my hand. I closed my eyes to listen to the music: Samuel Barber– Adagio for Strings. As the music enveloped me I allowed my mind to drift back sorrowfully to the previous night.

Kelly had been there again, in my bedroom for a short while. I hadn't really completely understood what she'd meant. I still wasn't sure whether it had been another vivid dream. All I knew was that she had told me what I had to do if there was to be any chance of her returning. I still couldn't believe it, yet even if it had been a dream,

I felt an instinctive desire to do as bidden and anyway, I excused myself, hadn't Kelly instructed me to do just that, take note of and use my dreams?

April cleared her throat and I opened my eyes to see her standing in front of me in a dress identical to the one in the shop window. I drew in my breath and whistled.

"Wow! That really suits you!"

"Thanks. My wine?" She took her glass and sipped before carefully sitting down next to me, then she quickly drained the rest of the amber liquid and plonked the empty glass on the sofa seat behind us."

"Hey, that's not a good idea; you might forget it's there. You know, I am just the tiniest bit concerned about the number of bottles of wine you and I have enjoyed together of late…"

"At the moment I don't care." She began stroking the back of my hair, my neck, then, finding no resistance, she leaned into me and kissed the side of my face. I sat very still and closed my eyes again. I felt her move and then her lips were on mine and her body was pressed against me. I didn't push her away but when the kiss ended I opened my eyes and looked into hers.

"You know how I feel about Kelly. I love you April but…"

"I don't care. I want you. Let me have tonight, please Peter? I will never ask again."

This was too easy. I had expected a bit of a challenge ahead this evening and certainly hadn't counted on April seducing me! Somehow it had the effect of resolving any feelings of guilt that might have got in the way. Still, she was my friend, I ought to come clean.

"April, I had this dream last night …"

"Yeah, so did I," she murmured, nibbling at my earlobe. "Stop

158

fretting; I can feel you want me."

This time when she kissed me I responded.

The next morning I woke to find myself sprawled on the floor, a duvet thrown over me and a cushion from the sofa beneath my head. The house was silent. I raised myself on one elbow and rubbed at a crick in my neck. There was a dull pain behind my eyes – a legacy from the two empty wine bottles on the table. I made a mental note not to partake of any more alcohol ever again. I got up, wrapping the duvet round the lower half of my naked body and went in search of my overnight bag in which I'd brought a change of clothing.

I found a note from April, attached to the fridge with a colourful magnet, shaped as a rainbow, when I went to fill the kettle to make coffee. It informed me she had gone to the library and would be back in time for lunch. There were eggs and bacon in the fridge if I was hungry. I decided I was not.

I spent the morning back at my own house, reading through the play, making minor alterations and re-printing the altered version. At about noon I was satisfied that all was ready for the meeting that evening, so I raided my fridge and larder for salads, ham, cheese, bread and fruit, and made my way back to April's home to make us some lunch. Everything was prepared and the table set when she returned just after 1:00 p.m. I'd been anxious things might be awkward and tense between us, or even worse that she might expect me to behave like a sentimental lover or something, but it was the same practical April who flung her coat over the back of the sofa and dumped some books on the dresser. She expressed genuine surprised delight at the meal waiting for her.

"I met Abigail in the library," she informed me, tearing off a piece of bread and lavishly applying butter. "She was on her coffee break. I remarked to her that I hadn't seen her when we were there before, perhaps because I didn't know her then, and she explained she'd been working in one of the back rooms scanning old newspapers and magazine articles onto microfilm and making new files for the computer, so they can clear space for storage. She seemed pleased to see me and I was quite touched because I don't think I was particularly friendly when we met. In fact I think I was a bit rude at her house – I didn't even thank her for her hospitality."

"She wouldn't hold that against you. She's a nice woman. Did she try to talk you into attending the book club meeting?"

"No, this is something much more interesting. She said she'd found an article which had reminded her somehow of your play – some local scandal about a writer having an affair and then his mistress mysteriously going missing. I think he was a murder suspect for a while."

I was impressed. "That *is* interesting. I shall have to go to the library and look it up sometime. Did you get a note of the details?"

"Better than that; she'd finished putting the article onto microfilm so she put the newspaper to one side and has given it to me for you to see. I thought it was really good of her, so I said you'd definitely go to the book club meeting next month."

"April, you didn't! When am I going to get the time to read the book they're studying before then?"

"Oh, I think you'll read this one," she declared. "Abigail asked me what sort of book you might like since it's her turn to choose this month and she hadn't decided what to read. Well, after seeing the article I made a suggestion. We looked up the writer's name and found the novel he wrote before the scandal broke. That's the book her circle will be reading this month. I lent a copy from the library for you. She's going to have to do a county-wide search to see if they have further copies in other libraries – the book's not particularly well-known."

She licked her fingers after finishing her piece of bread, got up from the table to collect the plates together and dump them in the sink. Then she went to get one of the books from the dresser and passed it to me. The paperback was white and had a black silhouette of a man standing in an arched doorway on the front, smoking a cigarette. The title, *Mandleknight's Chance,* was etched in thin, dark capital letters at the top of the cover and the author's name, B.

J. Terrace, was modestly placed at the bottom right-hand corner. I weighed the book in my hand, estimating that it probably consisted of some two hundred and sixty to three hundred pages. I figured I'd manage to work my way through it within a day or so.

"Thanks." I smiled my appreciation then went back to studying the novel.

I turned the book over to read the blurb on the back. I needn't have bothered though, as April immediately launched into a synopsis of the story.

Apparently a dashing young police officer was betrayed by his young, attractive wife with a work colleague. The hero's life fell apart as he lost his home, his job (along with any career prospects) and the motivation to do anything about it. However, he was eventually saved by his ex-wife appealing to him for help when her new partner was accused of embezzlement and fraud. He became a private detective, uncovering a plot against the government and ultimately finding evidence to prove that far from being innocent, the man he had set out to help was actually guilty.

I lifted a hand to halt April in her eagerness; I didn't want to know the end of the story before I'd even begun to read it. She laughed but heeded my request and went to fill the kettle for tea.

"April, about last night."

"Please don't Peter. I told you, I wanted it. I know the score. I have no intention of making your life difficult. We're still friends, okay?"

"Absolutely. I was just going to say thank you. It was nice."

"Good. Look I'm not going to lie, Peter. It's helped me a lot. I don't feel so desperately in love with you anymore."

"Oh thanks a lot! I suppose you've decided I was so magnificent, you're gay again."

She giggled, coming up behind me to put her arms about my

neck and kiss my head. "Of course not, silly. But I do think I might be bisexual."

I rolled my eyes, "Okay. Let's change the subject." She kissed my head again then released me, went back to the kettle to make the tea and placed a mug before me before sitting back down.

"So, how do we get to this mysterious crypt tonight? Were you really blindfolded when they took you the first time?"

"Yes but I've been back since with Mark Chapman to look over some of the notebooks and papers stored there. There's some interesting stuff. When Phillip Wells returns my dreams notebook I might add it to their collection."

"What happened about that? Did you go back and see him yet?"

"I did. I made an appointment one evening just before the end of term and told him I felt much better about things and wouldn't need too many more consultations, at least for a while. He said he'd hang onto my notebook for a week or two in case I had any more nightmares and changed my mind and I challenged him. I said, 'I suppose you want to keep it as evidence for the police – I heard you talking to them on the phone'."

April was thrilled, "You didn't!"

"I did. He didn't bother to deny it either. He eyed me disdainfully and told me I was fortunate that Kelly had contacted the police shortly after I'd reported her missing. They hadn't taken any of my concerns about her disappearance seriously after that, just kept a record, but as he'd made the call they assured him they would be looking into the case again."

"You haven't heard from them, though."

"Nope. I guess they just wanted to shut him up. I don't think they're really that interested. Although I must admit, I'll be happier when this is all over."

"Me too." Her face clouded over for a fraction of a second then the look was gone and I wondered whether I'd imagined it. "Look, I'm going to have a quick bath. We've got a couple of hours before we have to leave, haven't we?"

I looked at my watch. "Two and a half, to be precise. Change into something warm. They have heaters but the walk through the orchards is a bit bleak. I think I might make a start with this book."

I took my tea through to the lounge, as April headed for the bathroom, and made myself comfortable on the sofa. I looked at the publication date on the inside page and discovered the novel had been written some ten years previous. Disappointingly, there was no photograph or details of the author on the flyleaf so I ploughed straight in and was soon completely absorbed.

I was about a quarter of the way through the book, an hour later, and April still hadn't come back down. I wanted to discuss certain aspects of the story with her so I went upstairs and was about to knock tentatively on the bathroom door, ear bent close to the wood, when I heard a noise from within. It wasn't just the quiet splash and plop of water moving gently against the tub but the distinct sound of sobbing and I realised with a sinking heart that April was crying. I decided against disturbing and embarrassing her; I had a pretty good idea what the matter was, although her apparently cheerful mood and nonchalance in the kitchen had fooled me at the time. I went back downstairs wondering how to handle the situation. Perhaps it would be best to simply pretend ignorance of her distress.

I was about to retrieve the novel from where I'd left it next to her bag and other books on the dresser, when I caught sight of the old local newspaper. I picked it up, briefly examining the headline about a huge fire that had engulfed several houses and shops in the town that week. I opened the paper to search for the piece April had told me about and soon found the article with the heading: *Local Author helps police with their enquiries.* "I sympathise with you, mate, I really do," I said, glancing down briefly at the photo of the man beneath the report. To my utter amazement the face of the tall,

163

thin spy stared straight back at me – several years younger, perhaps, but it was definitely him. What's more, I suddenly realised as I studied the youthful profile that it was a photograph of the man I'd seen with Ella in my dream.

Chapter Eighteen

I hastily scribbled a message for April to tell her the meeting had been postponed and that I'd text her during the week then I left hurriedly with my manuscript, the novel and the newspaper stuffed into my overnight bag on top of my clothes and soap bag. I felt mean abandoning her but thought it for the best that she should have some time on her own under the circumstances. In the meantime, I intended to find out some more about Benjamin Terrace and I knew I would need help. However, I also realised that it wouldn't be fair to involve April any further for the time being. She was becoming too accustomed to having me around and I was concerned that when this business was over, she'd be lonely and unhappy and it would be my fault.

I had telephoned Frank, asking that the meeting be cancelled for a while, excusing myself by saying I'd had a few personal problems and needed a little more time to prepare, but promising this was a temporary situation and that I would soon be ready to make further arrangements to see everyone as planned. He promised to contact the rest of the group to let them know. I didn't want April to find me at my house so I'd then made a call to Mark Chapman, asking if he could put me up for a couple of nights. He was intrigued when I explained it had something to do with my writing and was therefore only too willing to oblige. I asked if it would inconvenience any plans he had with Caroline but he laughed and assured me that at present he was not expecting her company. He then added, chuckling, that since I'd be sleeping in his spare room there shouldn't be a problem even if she did turn up.

I wasn't sure how to approach the subject of my need to research the history and whereabouts of the novelist. I hadn't informed the group that I had been writing a play; they all still believed I'd be composing a particularly special poem. April had been my only confidante and, of course, I hadn't even told her everything.

When I'd recovered from my initial shock on seeing Ben Terrace's photograph, I'd decided Mark could be a useful ally. He'd smooth the way with the group into accepting April as a member and also help me to explain why it was necessary for me to create a poet rather than the poetry they were anticipating; I instinctively felt that he'd understand. He was undoubtedly perplexed when I showed him the play but he read through it before commenting.

"So, you've found a way around the poetry business then. You've created someone to write it for you."

"Not exactly," I then put the newspaper down on the table, folded open at the appropriate article. "Apparently my characters really exist!"

A momentary flicker of alarm crossed his inquiring eyes as they met mine before he read the article but when he finished he sat back on his chair, hands behind his head and surveyed me steadily.

"You really think they are the same people you had in mind for your play? I mean, it is a bit of a coincidence, the similarity in the stories, but perhaps you read it somewhere before and just didn't remember until now."

"Oh come on, Mark. You're not going to tell me you've started believing in coincidences like that!" I indicated the photograph. "That man is the same person I saw in the street the first time I had a vision of Kelly in my room."

"I see. I hadn't realised that."

"I haven't told you it all yet. That was the man I saw coming from my house when it had been completely redecorated and refurnished without my knowledge or consent. He also took my coat – I can't say stole because he returned it – from the train the night we had Pheobe's send off. I'm assuming that was something to do with the poetry book, since it was the day we went to get it, but he seems reluctant to communicate with me directly. It's all too strange for words and I don't understand how I came to write about him and his affairs or what his game is but he seems pretty elusive and I believe I'm going to need some help to find him."

"Certainly I'll do everything I can to assist you. I have a friend in the force; perhaps he'll be able to throw some light on this bloke's whereabouts since he was once a copper, although perhaps this is other-worldly, if you get my meaning."

"I don't know. I haven't seen him 'shatter' so I think seeking your friend's assistance would be a good start. There's something else I need to talk to you about. I want to introduce somebody else to the group and I'd be grateful for your support."

I explained about April and he listened attentively, letting out a breath in a long, low whistle once I'd finished. "You're telling me you believe your wife instructed you to have sex with another woman? A woman who undoubtedly was, and still is, emotionally involved with you, however you choose to dress it up?

"Hmm. I know, it does sound a bit fantastic but it's true."

"You don't think your dream was simply wish-fulfillment. I mean, you said yourself it's been a long time?"

"All I can think is that if I have made a mistake, and I don't believe I have, Kelly will understand. As you said, it's been a long time. My only regret is that April is hurting and I wouldn't want to cause that sort of unhappiness to my worst enemy let alone someone that I care about."

Mark made no comment but later, as I lay staring into the dark in the tiny spare bedroom, I re-ran the conversation in my head, then tried to imagine how April must be feeling alone at her house. Part of me wanted to be there with her, comforting her and making everything alright. Yes, I did care about her and, if I was honest with myself, the previous night's activities had only served to deepen that affection. The sooner Kelly was home, I decided, the better for everyone.

Unlike all the best detective novels and thrillers, Mark's friend did not 'come up with the goods'. It was not that he couldn't locate any records of Ben Terrace, it was just that he was unwilling even to try. It was confidential information. We were not relatives of Terrace and we were unable to give sufficient reason for him to consider taking the time. Whatever favour Mark had been hoping to call in hadn't been deemed worthy of such repayment. My friend apologised profusely and we discussed where we should go from there.

We searched the internet but to no avail – there wasn't even reference to the novel or any other novel written by Terrace. We discussed the different ways in which people researched family trees but decided it would all take much too long. We eventually came to the conclusion that we should go ahead with the meeting and the play and discuss Terrace and the newspaper article and novel when it seemed appropriate. The group would surely come up with some sort of solution.

I made the call to Frank later that night and we decided the meeting should go ahead early the following evening. I then switched on my mobile to text April, reluctant to telephone because that would be too immediate. I wasn't surprised to see there was already a text from her from the previous day, asking me to call her. Despite my reluctance to talk to her, I owed it to her to do as she requested and I keyed in her number with some trepidation; I didn't want to argue.

To my dismay April sounded nervous and upset. She explained that she had disturbed an intruder in her house in the early hours of the morning and had been unable to relax or sleep since the police had left. I promised to get to her house as soon as possible and hurriedly explained to Mark before grabbing my belongings and setting off. He asked if I wanted him to accompany me, but I refused and he didn't argue – I was glad of that. Things were complicated enough without having a spectator along.

April cautiously peered through her curtains before coming to the door but flung herself into my arms as soon as it was open. Guiltily, I hugged her to me and guided her through to the lounge to tell me everything. She explained she'd been woken by a noise downstairs and had descended thinking perhaps I had returned. Instead she found the room in darkness and a dark figure with a torch emptying her cupboards and drawers. She was groping frantically for the light switch when the intruder must have seen her and sprang in her direction, pushing past to get out of the front door and away. She didn't see the person's face and was unable to give the police many details except to say that from the sheer height of the person she had believed the intruder to be a man, although his frame had been far from bulky. I felt goose bumps raise the hair on my forearms and back of my neck and decided to bring April up to date with everything, beginning at when I'd recognised the photograph in the newspaper article and culminating in my fruitless research with Mark Chapman.

"Do you think it was Benjamin Terrace in my house?" She asked, a note of anxiety creeping into her voice.

"I wouldn't rule it out. I'll stay here tonight in case he comes back," I reassured her. 'We don't particularly want your house ransacked like mine. Perhaps he's looking for the poetry book. Pity I wasn't here on your couch, I could have surprised him and discovered what he's up to."

April chuckled and I looked at her feeling slightly aggrieved that she should find this funny.

"I just had an image of you hurling yourself at him in a rugby tackle as he made for the door!"

I looked down at my own somewhat slender frame and remembering my modest height, couldn't resist a wry grin in acknowledgment of her perception.

"Well, there's to be a meeting tomorrow and we're going to try out the play. Perhaps we'll talk to Frank and the others about

Terrace afterwards."

By mutual agreement, I slept next to April that night, fully clothed on top of the duvet, while she slumbered underneath. She'd asked if I'd sleep in her bed with her not to have sex, but because she was nervous of being alone again and she'd agreed to the compromise.

"I care for you deeply, April, you must know that and I'm worried I might be tempted again. Under different circumstances we'd be in a proper relationship by now and if we aren't careful someone is going to get hurt. I don't want that and I don't think you do either." She agreed and we changed the subject, discussing instead the play and which people from the group would be suitable for the different roles.

"I suppose everyone could do something, even if they are only extras in the café scene or wandering along the river banks."

"Who do you think for Ben? What about Tony?"

"I think you should play Ben."

"Me? I thought I might be James …"

"No you should be Ben. Or maybe the stranger; I think he, rather than James, saved Ben's marriage. Tony can play James. I'd like to be Ella."

"I think Frank could possibly play James. I'll probably just direct. I don't think there will be a part for everyone, there's fourteen or fifteen in that group and you'll be adding to our number of course."

"The rest can be audience. Does the crypt have a very good performance area? I still think you should, without a doubt, be Ben or the stranger. You can direct as well."

"Maybe. I have to go to sleep now. Sorry, I'm all in."

We settled down and I was drifting off to sleep when April suddenly sprang up in bed, listening. "Peter, I think there's someone in the house again."

I listened. She was right; I could hear the distinct soft tread of another human being and things being moved about in the room below. I grabbed my glasses and told April to stay where she was, then I crept downstairs. Sure enough the tall, thin stranger was rifling through April's papers and possessions. I flicked the light switch and cleared my throat loudly at the same time. I had already pulled the lounge door closed so the intruder had no easy means of escape. He froze, half bent to retrieve something from the floor, as light flooded the room.

"Hello Ben." I could see now that the man was dressed completely in black, including a balaclava that covered all but his eyes. He looked ridiculously like a four-legged spider. He slowly stood up straight and pulled the balaclava from his head.

"How do you know who I am?"

"I'll ask the questions if you don't mind. What are you doing in my friend's home? Are you looking for the poetry book?" He looked startled but nodded.

"Well, I can tell you now it isn't here. Why do you want it?"

"It belongs to me."

"I beg to differ. I found it at a second-hand bookshop and I purchased it. Therefore it's mine, possession being nine tenths of the law as they say."

"Then I'll refund your money. It should never have been at the bookshop. I wrote those poems. It belongs to me."

The door was pushed open from behind me, momentarily causing my attention to shift as April entered the room. It was barely a few seconds but enough time for Terrace to dart from the room to the kitchen. I shouted in surprise and we followed close on his heels, but he had the back door unlocked and was out and over the garden fence before I could catch him. He was extremely agile for a man I believed to be in his late forties, early fifties. I made a mental note to keep myself in equally good shape in future; I'd like to be able to bound over two metre high fences without so much as a grunt.

"I'm sorry Peter. I shouldn't have come down. I could hear voices and there was no sound of a struggle so I assumed it was safe and I was curious to see who you were talking to."

"Never mind, at least part of the mystery is solved. He's the author of the poetry book. I didn't get to find out anything else though and I'm particularly intrigued as to why he's so desperate to get it back." I closed the back door and relocked it. It seemed pointless to call the police and fortunately Terrace hadn't managed to disturb too many of April's things. We decided to go back to bed.

"Peter, do you think Ben Terrace has anything to do with Kelly's disappearance?" April asked the question once we were comfortably settled back in our respective places on the bed.

"I don't know but I intend to find out," I replied. "Now get some rest. Goodnight." April turned onto her side and was gently snoring within minutes. However, I couldn't stop wondering about the intruder and it was some time before I was able to sleep myself.

Chapter Nineteen

"I believe if you absorb emotional pain you become bitter, inwardly cynical, and part of your spirit will stay at that place where you suffered." My hands were behind my back as I paced up and down. "At first you will constantly play recordings of old conversations like a tape recorder in your head, gradually adding wished for alterations to those discussions, attempting to ease the agony by imagining yourself as a nobler and wiser person." I stopped walking and looked up from the ground. "Eventually those recordings will fade, but the belief that you behaved better than you actually did, will remain as part of the healing process.

"I sincerely believe the hurt must go somewhere for you to survive if you wish to remain true to yourself and alive to all that life has to offer, so I tried to release the agony of betrayal in the poetry I wrote."

"That's some speech and, I might add, it's not in the script!"

"That's because I've only just come to understand that it's how Ben felt, the explanation he would give if he could articulate his reasons for the way in which the poetry degenerated. I don't think he ever intended his work – I mean this particular little book of poems – to be published or indeed even to be seen by other people. Remember how he insisted to Ella that he didn't even like poetry?"

"But she knew about the poems, she must have from her protest! How do you suppose it came to be in the book shop then?" April frowned, trying to make sense of it all.

"I don't know. I'll ask if I ever get an opportunity."

"Great! You're talking as if your fictional character really was the author," Frank interposed. "I'm even beginning to believe it myself! You're right about this play, Peter. It could work, although I have to admit to having had certain reservations when you first introduced the idea. To an outsider, who hasn't studied the subjects we have, even using poetry would seem peculiar enough – but a play!"

Frank was clearly excited. He was seated on the bench on which I had previously rested when I'd seen Kelly in the crypt. He had the poetry book at his side, the table to his left and the floor around him was covered by notebooks and papers from the cabinet. Various members of the philosophy group sat on cushions or benches around the edge of the area on which we were standing to perform. Mark and I exchanged meaningful glances at Frank's comment and I was aware of April's eyes on the pair of us. It was time to come clean.

However, when I began to confess that actually Ben Terrace did exist, was undoubtedly the author of the book and that we had proof, the old man held up a hand.

"This is all very interesting Peter but we must go on. The time is right, I can sense it, do you agree?" He included everybody in this last question.

He was right. Something in the atmosphere had shifted slightly, an almost imperceptible change, yet we were all now aware of it so we took our positions again and continued. Sarah, one of the two older women that I barely knew, made a timid suggestion that we feel free to improvise whenever it seemed appropriate, that we should all rely on our instincts and inner senses. There was a general murmur of approval and people nodded their agreement.

The play then began to evolve and take on a certain existence almost of its own, as if it were not a play at all but reality. The air seemed charged with electricity and almost fizzed and crackled as we acted out the parts. We came to the riverside scene and April, as Ella, was weeping with true sincerity. I actually felt rage well up inside me at Ella's resistance to my proposals and I knew I was becoming hurtful and defiant.

"You are in love with me, why are you doing this?" I almost screamed at April and was shocked at the intensity of my emotions, suddenly knowing that it wasn't April now but Ella looking back at me as Ben. I was relieved when I could step aside and allow Tony to approach and comfort the distressed woman. Everyone present was by now deeply engrossed in the performance.

"I believe you will walk away from this, and one day you will meet someone else who is free to love you as you deserve…"

"Nooo!" We stopped, stunned into silence by the distraught wail from the unexpected intruder.

As one, we turned to the heavy oak door of the crypt which now stood wide open. Ben Terrace, himself, stood framed in the entrance.

"Why would you tell her to leave me? Why would you do that? I've never done anything to you!"

He strode across the room but instead of making for Tony he took hold of me by the front of my shirt, shouting into my face in his desperation. Several male members of the group leapt forward to take hold of and restrain Ben. He was very strong and they held on with some effort. I fell back onto the floor as he released me and was getting back up onto my feet, straightening my clothes, as he began to shout furiously.

"Let go of me, let go!"

"She isn't Nina, your first wife, Ben. She deserves to be loved for herself."

The voice was quiet but firm and the unhappy man ceased struggling, his arms dropping limply to his sides as he stared across the room; the men released him and we all turned as one to see

175

Kelly, my lovely, serious wife standing there, her attention riveted on my attacker.

"She loves me." His voice was strained with emotion.

"I know but so does Sandra and you do actually care for your wife for herself and not as a replacement of someone you've lost. Let Ella go."

"It will hurt her. I don't want her to hurt the way I did. She loves me. Let me have time to make everything right. You do love me don't you, Ella?" He had left me now, stepping forward to fall at April's feet, taking hold of her hands and staring desperately up into her face, which had become swollen and flushed from crying. She began to nod slowly but Kelly intervened again.

"She is not Ella anymore than Ella was Nina. Your lover has moved on with her life." Kelly went on, calm, unwavering. "I am not Nina either, and never could be." She paused and pointed across the room. "That is April and she loves Peter."

April sat very still, watching, as the desperate man suddenly snatched his hands away from her as if he had just been burnt. He rocked back on his haunches, put his hands on his head, raking disconsolately at his hair, looking first at her and then at Kelly.

"But, but surely Peter is *your* husband. You told me so!"

"Yes, Ben, and April's in love with Peter," Kelly persisted. "It happens. They are friends and it couldn't be helped. She's in love with Peter but she will walk away and let him go because she knows he is married to me and that he loves me. And I love him. She knows it's the right thing to do, just as Ella knew it was right to leave you for Sandra's sake."

"I don't know what to do. I don't know how to cope with this."

Kelly's eyes shone with compassion at his anguish. I felt everybody in the room must be holding their breath.

176

"Let it go, Ben. Let Ella go. Let Nina go. Return to your present wife; she needs your love. Sandra's still waiting for you to return." Kelly gave Ben a moment for the words to take effect, and then she continued. "It's in the past, too long ago for you to continue to suffer; that's why I took the book. I wanted to help. Let go of the poetry. Let go of the past and release me. Accept that Nina never loved you and forgive her."

"She destroyed me. The pain was too much. I can't ever fall in love again."

"You do love, though." Her words were still quiet, but determined.

"It's the only way I can have relationships, if I don't allow myself to fall in love," he persisted.

"What gives you the right to use other people to make you feel better? You're just a player, a womanizer!" April suddenly hurled the accusation at him.

I bit my lip in shame, not able to look at her, wondering whether the comment had been directed at me too. Surely I was no better than Ben in that respect?

"I just want to prove to myself that I can be everything to someone, just as she was to me. I really believed she loved, needed and wanted me as much as I did her and all the time she was playing me for a fool!"

"It isn't fair to treat somebody else the way you feel you were treated, just because you manage to inspire that kind of feeling in another person. You can't go deliberately causing someone else pain, just because you got hurt!" I'd found my voice at last, relieved that this was not what I'd been doing the night I'd made love to April. I had never meant to cause her pain. This man, on the other hand, seemed to be caught in a destructive cycle; in his own way he wasn't just punishing other women for the way his first wife had treated him, he was making them suffer because they had been foolish enough to trust as he had trusted and in the process he was punishing himself.

Kelly spoke again. "Nina didn't destroy you, Ben. It's your choice that you don't fall completely in love and that's okay, but you can still exalt in the memory of what it was like while you *were* in love. You can still accept the fact that you, Ben Terrace, experienced this wonderful emotion and, if you do, it can light up the whole universe for you and fill the world with music. As I said, you may not be *in* love with Sandra in the same way as you were with Nina but you have to admit that you *do* love her."

For long seconds the scene was frozen in a tableau.

"I don't have to fall completely in love again?"

"No. I believed that was the answer too, at first, but it isn't. I'm sorry I got it so wrong. I know now that all you have to do, Ben, is to allow yourself to love faithfully and accept being loved in return."

"You're right; I do love Sandra, in my own way."

"I know you do. It's enough."

Ben slowly got up from his knees, totally oblivious of everybody else in the room now. He crossed over to the bench where the little poetry book lay and picked it up, leafing slowing through the pages. Suddenly the tortured expression faded from his face and he smiled sadly. He turned and walked towards Kelly, holding out the book. I wanted to shout for him to stop, to tell him that if he touched her she would vanish but my voice caught in my throat and I was rooted to the spot, obliged to watch the scene unraveling before me along with everyone else.

Ben halted in front of Kelly and held out the book. To my amazement she smiled into his eyes and took it. She held it in her hands for a second then it seemed to burst into flames; except there was no fire. The whole room shone with the brilliance of the combustion. In a moment all that was left in her hands was dust and she allowed this to trickle between her fingers to the floor, her eyes never once leaving Ben's face. There was a collective sigh from those present in the crypt.

"Thank you."

Ben gently reached forward as if to caress Kelly's face, but let his hand drop at the last moment. I think I understood then what women found so appealing about him, and I noticed for the first time that rather than seeming sinister, his face was quite good-looking in a brooding, romantic kind of way. As we watched he turned and strode purposely towards the door without looking back. The heavy oak thudded back into place as he left the crypt.

The previously hushed room erupted into excited conversation. Tony gave April an impulsive hug and I smiled as she hugged him back, then looked into his face and kissed him full on the mouth. He didn't seem in the least disturbed by this and took her enthusiastically into his arms to return the kiss. For the moment at least, it seemed I was forgotten.

I looked back to the place where the illusion of my pretty, serene, wise young wife had stood, expecting the mirage to be gone again, my hope vanquished, this time forever. She was, however, still there looking at me. Our eyes met and for the moment it was if we were completely alone in the crypt.

Kelly smiled wistfully and then stepped forward into my arms.

Chapter Twenty

A week later we all enjoyed a wonderful bonfire barbeque, in the orchard near to the crypt. Everybody was there. It was a Sunday afternoon and the weather was warm – almost as if summer had decided to visit entirely for our benefit. It was a good opportunity to become better acquainted with the lesser known members of the group, as well as catch up with those who had become dear friends. Kelly sat close to me and every now and then we would gaze into each other's eyes and then kiss. April wandered over to us arm in arm with Mark. I frowned and shook my head, smiling and April had the grace to blush, although my male teaching colleague looked totally unapologetic.

"What happened to young Tony?

"Oh, he's over there with Marcia. More his age, I think."

"And Caroline?" I grinned as Mark released April and stuffed his hands into his pockets.

"It would seem her ex-husband is back on the scene. This young lady has offered to console me for the afternoon and perhaps even longer. We shall see. I didn't think you'd mind, under the circumstances."

"You'd better be good to my friend or you'll have me to answer to!"

"Good for you!" This comment came from Kelly as she and

April exchanged smiles. I sensed the two women would become close friends before much longer and I was glad.

"We're off to get some mulled wine; can we get anything for the two of you?"

"I think we're just fine, thanks." My attention was taken up with my wife again and the pair took the hint and left us to it. After another tender embrace I leaned back on my elbow.

"It's time we discussed April. Every time I've brought up the subject you've found an excuse to avoid it. You know I slept with her…"

"It was the right thing to do. You needed comfort and release and it was necessary to create a triangle similar to that with Ben, Ella and Sandra, for him to be able to see the truth."

"How could it be right to use April?"

"You know you weren't using her. You genuinely care for her and you wanted to give her the opportunity to express her feelings. If I hadn't been able to get back to you, I expected you to make a life with her."

"Weren't you afraid you might lose me?"

"I could never lose you, Peter. You're in love with me. That's why I could reach you and how you were able to empathise with Ben and write the play. That's why you understood the poetry. I'm sorry I left you for so long. There's something I have to tell you. I became involved with Ben for a while."

"Yeah, I kind of assumed that. Did you, do you still love him?"

The question hadn't really been serious but she unnerved me when she paused momentarily to think before replying. My heart began to pound so hard that my ears seemed full of the sound and my chest became tight so that it was difficult to breathe properly.

"I felt sorry for him and I think I mistook that for love. I felt unhappy with my world and he made me feel that life had a purpose. The more time I spent with him, the less visible you seemed to be. I thought it was because you didn't need me and so I began to believe I didn't want to stay with you. Ben seemed to offer a way out. The trouble was, when it came to the crunch neither Ben nor I could really make the commitment. Ben told me not to worry, that he wasn't in love with me anyway – he read me some of the poetry as proof. He said that he enjoyed my company enough for us to still be able to make a go of it together. It wasn't how it sounds; he wasn't being kind and romantic, he was brutally candid, cold even.

"The day I left you, I went to see him and tell him I'd decided to make a life on my own. To be honest, I intended to wait for a while and give you time to realise how much I meant to you. When the time felt right I would have then asked for your help to put our marriage back together. I even thought about us having children and that's when I wrote the letter. I left it hidden at a bed and breakfast place where I'd been staying.

"Anyway, when I explained to Ben that I couldn't be with him, he was furious and said that all women were the same. I fled from his house and took the poetry book with me. He ran after me. I was out of his sight for a few moments so I stuffed the poetry book into a box of books which were outside a shop being refurbished and refitted with shelving. I kept on running but of course by the time he caught me the book was gone. He was really angry – I'll never forget it. I'd got as far as the riverside at Westgate gardens and he grabbed hold of me by the wrists. His eyes were blazing but he didn't say a word and for a brief moment I thought he would kill me. I screwed up my eyes and recited the last piece of melancholy poetry I remembered reading from the book because I thought it might bring him back to his senses – I said the words as if they were a prayer; poetry is so powerful you know, I think because it expresses the truth in a way that ordinary prose can't. Suddenly I found myself in a wonderful but strange place, full of clouds and colours and goodness knows what. I don't know what happened to Ben after that.

"I eventually discovered I could reach certain members of the group through dreams at certain times of the year and gradually I worked on finding a way to communicate with you."

"So you really were on some other plane of existence?"

"Incredible as that sounds, I do actually believe I was. I don't really know for sure and it's difficult to remember much detail. All I can tell you is that I wasn't particularly aware of the passing of time. I was sometimes conscious of certain dates because other people in the place reminded me, although I couldn't for the world tell you who any of them were or what they looked like. Somehow it didn't feel as if I was away for any length of time at all because in a way I was always here too."

"What about your appearances?"

"Dream-walking."

"Oh! Do you mean you were aware you were in a dream? I think I did something like that!"

"Not quite. Although we, the guides and I, were helping you to join us for short spells and could communicate with you at certain times, when you were asleep or in the right frame of mind. Sometimes I could see your memories and feel your emotions and then I was afraid for you. No, when I say I was dream-walking I mean I was 'walking' into other people's 'dream-states'. Again, people had to be in a certain frame of mind to be able to see me– open and accepting, searching even – that's why the philosophy group was so helpful. You know how friends telephone, or visit, just at a time when their support is most needed and they joke about 'sending' vibes? It's probably closer to the truth than people realise!"

"Wow! So these 'guides', are they the spirits of dead people?"

Kelly shrugged. "All I know for certain is that, while I was with them, I felt they were somehow familiar to me and they seemed to know me intimately. I knew intuitively that they had all of our best interests at heart. Being with them made me consider the possibility they might be angels. No, don't laugh, I'm serious! All I can say is that whoever they are, they are immeasurably good and the kindest, wisest beings you could possibly imagine."

Rather than satisfying my curiosity, April's explanation served to rouse it further.

"Look, I know I smiled a little when you said about the angels but I really don't disbelieve you, not after everything that's happened. Tell me a bit more about the dream-walking."

"Well I'm sorry to be so vague but I don't know much more. It's just as mysterious and remarkable to me as it is to you, and I was there! As I understand it, dream-walking was an ancient tradition rediscovered by a man, some sort of spiritualist, in the 19th Century and forgotten again after his death, when his journals were destroyed in a fire. I can't remember his name – I think I read it somewhere or perhaps someone told me. Anyway, it's said he's buried in a secret cave, beneath wood but between water and land and that at certain times of the year it is possible to tap into his powers or 'gifts'. That's what I think I did and the guides, through you, assisted me."

"I seem to remember a peculiar dream, being at the place you describe – some sort of cave!"

"I think it all has something to do with the physical balance of emotions and nature. Ben's unhappiness, and inability to move on with his life, was impacting on too many people. I'm not sure. Perhaps it's just a theory and I've got it all wrong but I sort of believe it has something to do with that."

"How did you get to know Ben?"

"I'd found his novel at the library while I was looking for new poetry books. I'm really crazy about poetry now. I don't know why but the novel intrigued me and I was reading, sitting on a bench near the river at Westgate gardens. I looked up and he was gazing at me intently, yet I wasn't concerned because he had such a gentle expression in his eyes. Then he introduced himself as the author of the book I was reading and we got talking."

"I see. Did you have sex during your involvement?" I struggled to keep my voice calm.

"Does it matter so very much?"

"I'm just thinking perhaps you encouraged me to sleep with April as a way of compensating for something."

She laughed then and embraced me fiercely. "No, Peter. I didn't have sex with Ben. Neither do I believe a marriage should end because one of the parties has sex with someone else. If the marriage is strong it can survive just about anything, although outside involvement is a symptom of problems which can, and does in many cases, damage relationships beyond repair. There has to be trust. That's something we need to discuss at some future date so there can be no further misunderstandings. For now, let's just enjoy being together again for a while."

April and Mark had returned with glasses of drinks and food on trays. They sat down on the edge of the picnic rug we had spread on the grass, pushing aside our discarded coats. Mark idly picked a sprig of grapes from his plate and casually remarked, "You two were deep in conversation – I suppose you still have a lot to talk about. I have to admit, despite what you've already told us, Kelly, we still have a few questions of our own, if you don't mind?"

"If I can explain anything, I will."

"Peter's house – I take it you gave Ben the key?"

"Well, actually he took it from my bag without my knowledge. He was looking for the poetry book when he turned the house upside down. He must have thought I'd somehow got it home."

"But the paint and graffiti– I don't see how he could know the symbol on the shop where you'd left the book without being able to guess where to find it?"

"Ahh, that artwork was nothing to do with him. I needed outside help for that, among other things."

186

We all three stared at her in astonishment. "But who?"

"My Mum."

April's expression was immediately full of sympathy. "Oh Kelly, I was so sorry to hear about her death…"

I pulled my wife to me and stroked her hair but she chuckled self-consciously and pulled herself out of my arms for a moment to look up at me, her eyes full of mischief.

"What?"

"She isn't really dead. I managed to convince her to help me through dreams and afterwards appearing, as I did with you. She really does love me an awful lot and it took a huge step of faith and a great deal of courage for her to do as I asked and convince my father to play along with it."

We were all transfixed, gaping at my wife in shock.

"Of course she hated being a graffiti artist and was convinced she'd be caught and blamed for the 'burglary' too but she'd promised me she'd do it, when I made one of my appearances. I hadn't realised that she'd left your house in such a panic that she drove into your mini. Then, of course, she felt mortified about that, so contrived to buy you a new car. She made my poor father pretend to be you and go to the garage and forge your signature. She always could wrap him round her little finger but fraud!" She put her hand over her mouth for a second, "I never thought in a million years she'd be able to get him to do anything like that – he must have been a nervous wreck!"

I felt that it obviously hadn't yet occurred to my wife the extent to which she had caused distress and anxiety to the people who loved her the most. There had been times when I believe I had been on the very brink of madness myself. I just couldn't comprehend how she could deliberately have me believe her mother was dead, and afterwards just laugh about it.

"Why would you do that to us, Kelly? Why make them lie and have me believe Maureen was dead? That was cruel and unnecessary." I kept my voice low and controlled but she could tell I was extremely upset.

"It *was* necessary to make you believe that the dreams were more than your mind's inventions, that you weren't having some sort of psychotic episode. I'm sorry. You simply *had* to believe in the supernatural element of what was going on or I would never have been able to get back!"

She looked so worried and distressed at my reaction that my anger melted away and I eventually took her in my arms again. I wasn't sure I completely agreed with her, and I'd certainly be having words with my in-laws. Nevertheless, I could understand how they must have felt and knew that in their position I probably would have done the same; I too had been ready and prepared to do almost anything to get Kelly back.

Once she was confident that I'd forgiven her she settled with her back against my chest so I could still hold her but she could talk to April and Mark at the same time.

"So, what are you going to do now you are back apart from enjoying being with Peter again?"

I hadn't expected Mark to ask anything of such a personal nature but I was glad he had because I was wondering the same thing myself, anxious that before she left Kelly had been depressed about not having employment."

"Oh, I don't know. Try to find work, I suppose, maybe go to art college. I might write a novel about everything that happened. I'd change names, of course, but it would have to be a work of fiction because nobody would ever believe the truth."

I could tell from her expression that April relished the idea even less than I did but Mark was intrigued.

"Do you know, that's quite an interesting project," he enthused. "If you did write the novel, what would be the title? I might enjoy a read."

"Well, since it involves complicated love relationships between various trios, I think it would have to be *Triangles*," Kelly said.

Lightning Source UK Ltd.
Milton Keynes UK
25 November 2009

146686UK00001B/46/P